DEATH AT THE BRITISH EMBASSY

BY

NORMA MOSS

New Generation **Publishing**

For

Peter Moss,
Whose idea it was,
Leaning over that Bangkok balcony,
Happy memories

CHAPTER ONE

After the body was found in the embassy lake, those in the know at the British embassy were sure that it had been meant to be discovered sooner than it was. It seemed almost certain that its discovery had been planned to take place during the Ploenchit Fair when it would have involved maximum publicity of the worst kind for the embassy. However, having settled deep into the mud, helped perhaps by the play of the ornamental waterfall and then wedged by a stone, it had not surfaced on that day and would probably not have been found even when it was but for an unforeseen intervention, a canine adventure.

The ambassador's dog Pooky made a habit of chasing the Gurkha guards' cat, (whose name is unrecorded) whenever it came within her vision although, more often than not, the dog was routed by the cat's imperturbability. On this occasion, however, maddened by the dog, the usually phlegmatic feline swarmed up a tree just by the lake which occupies an area of about 2 metres right behind the Residence. There it clung to a branch and spitting down at the excited dog, provoked that creature into a sudden delusion about its abilities and she began to climb the tree as well. Halfway up, the delusion was shattered and the dog fell noisily into the lake, displacing the stone and bringing the body wedged under it to the surface.

The splash was heard by Ram Bahadur, the Gurkha guard and nominal owner of the cat, who came running to the lake. What he saw there caused him to yell at the top of his voice and brought a couple of his cohorts rushing to the scene, followed by the gardeners who were still clearing up the debris from the Ploenchit Fair.

Together they stood at the water's edge, pointing and whispering, while the body, which seemed to be lying on its side, bobbed gently to and fro in the water. Despite its muddy appearance, none of them doubted for a moment that it was a human body.

By the time Tony Walcott, the Admin. Officer, arrived at the lake, the scene was gruesome indeed for Pooky, the dog, had managed to stir up the mud in the lake which was only about a metre deep and this had brought the body trapped in its sticky embrace further to the surface. Tony spoke briskly to the Gurkhas: "We have to get it out of the water. Damn it!" he added, as Pooky came towards him and had a good shake, spattering his trousers with muddy water, before she raced off across the grass to the Residence. The cat, after surveying the scene, came slowly and carefully down the tree, regarded everyone there with its usual contemptuous expression, then tail held high, conceding nothing, it departed towards the Gurkha quarters on the north side of the compound.

The Gurkhas regarded the mud covered object lying submerged in the lake with revulsion. They knew only too well what was going to happen next and none of them were prepared to volunteer for the job.

"Go on then", said Tony Walcott briskly, "we have got to get that thing out of there, see who it is for christ's sake." Those last few words he addressed more or less to himself.

The Gurkhas, undeceived by the plural pronoun, hesitated and talked in Gurkhali among themselves. Then Ram Bahadur rolled up his trousers, took off his shoes and strode into the water, his toes squelching in the mud. The water was almost up to his shoulders for he, like most of his tribe, was short and stocky. All around him there were water lilies and lotus bloomed pink and white but neither he nor anyone else noticed

6

the beautiful flowers; all eyes were trained on the body which now, disturbed by the Gurkha's advent, bobbed more energetically. He bent and seized it by an outstretched arm and clenching his teeth, dragged it trailing in his wake back to the bank.

"Christ what a smell!" muttered Tony Walcott, as he steeled himself to bend and examine the corpse that Ram Bahadur dropped in front of him, much as a retrieving dog might lay its kill at its master's feet.

Everywhere else on the embassy compound that morning, things were going on much as usual. At the Residence, the ambassador Maurice Pentland Hervey, having regretfully declined a proper English breakfast (his ulcers were playing up), had finished a frugal repast of fruit and tea with his wife Claire and their daughters Candida and Emma who were visiting from Britain.

"Where is Pooky?" he asked, since the dog was usually to be found ogling the sausages and ham with a hopeful eye and an inquisitive nose. His elder daughter Candida shrugged. "That dog is spoiled rotten", she said, "you and Mother haven't spent much time on training her."

"Darling", Claire Pentland Hervey said, "she is only a puppy".

"Catch them young and break their spirit , that's Candida's motto for people and animals", put in Emma who loved to rile her older sister. "It's probably also the motto of that dour but good looking Mr Jerry Barton of the Drug Enforcement Section. I've noticed our Candida mooning over him."

"Oh, you are such a little bitch", said Candida, "anyway, you're just jealous because he treats you like the child you are."

Sensing conflict as the sisters glared at each other,

with unfailing diplomatic good sense, the ambassador kissed his wife and daughters goodbye, and departed at his usual unhurried pace to his office which looked out on Wireless Road. Normally, he went by the back door, cutting across the grass, which would have brought him within view of the lake and then it might have been he who discovered the body. Today, however, mindful of an imminent visit by the diplomatic inspectors from Whitehall, he wanted to have a look at the facade of the flats to the left of the Residence and so he went out of the front door. As he strolled out of the Residence he glanced at the massive figure of Queen Victoria which sat with its back to him, looking imperially out towards Ploenchit Road where, as usual despite the early hour, the traffic sat unmoving.

"Oh, Bangkok!" he muttered to himself and hoped fervently that they would not have too many problems with the Diplomatic Inspectors; the Queen was due to visit Thailand and all he wanted was to get a knighthood and retire peacefully to the Cotswolds. He also wished his daughters got on better with one another and he certainly hoped neither of them was really falling in love with Jerry Barton. Jerry was a first class officer but the ambassador seriously doubted whether he was good husband material.

Mr Pentland Hervey's departure by the front door was followed by the arrival of Pooky from the back, covered in mud and slime, her plumed tail and feathery hair clinging wetly to her body. Khun Somchai, the butler, was the first to catch sight of her as she tried to slink along the wide veranda and he called out to her, hoping to divert her from dripping all over the carpets in the living room.

Emma Pentland Hervey came out and caught sight of the dog who had stopped dead in its tracks and now attempted to wave a guilty but propitiatory tail as it caught sight of its young mistress.

"Why, wherever have you been Pooky?" she called, "oh, you are a dirty, naughty doggie! You're lucky Candida didn't see you."

Pooky had never before shown any propensity to swim in the lake and was probably already regretting the impulse as she was seized and hurried away for a proper bath; she was washed clean and tied up for the rest of the morning to ponder her misdoing and thus ended Pooky's adventure.

For everybody else in the embassy and elsewhere in Bangkok, the nightmare she had unleashed was only just beginning.

CHAPTER TWO

To almost everyone in Bangkok it would be inconceivable that anyone should even think of using the Ploenchit Fair for any thing other than its purpose which was to raise as much money as possible for all sorts of worthy charities. Yet, after the body was found in the lake, it seemed that this year, much more had been meant to take place than had been planned by those officially in charge of the festivities.

Sarah Barrett, for many years the organising genius behind not only the Ploenchit Fair but several other charities that disbursed money to the needy in Bangkok, was the wife of the Chairman of Bedrock UK, a very wealthy and large corporation. This position, combined with her undoubted talent for organisation and fund raising (nobody dared say no to Mrs Barrett) had made her the President of the Committee for UK Charities which she ruled with a rod of iron.

When, after the event, the embassy began to think that the run-up to the Ploenchit Fair might have been used to suss out the grounds, and the Fair itself to pass information, this discovery was kept under wraps and was certainly not imparted to the ladies of the Committee for UK Charities. It would have caused Mrs Barrett and her Committee major distress for the fair was the pivot of their existence; hours of unremitting committee work under the patronage of the British ambassador's wife, punctuated by endless cups of coffee, went into each year's successful fair. The Ploenchit Fair is an annual event in Bangkok and the preparations for this gala event take almost a year to organise. The several highly placed ladies who serve on Sarah Barrett's committee spend the better part of that year bludgeoning businessmen and the wealthy and influential, into donating as much as possible to the fair. The success of the event is undisputed, raising as much as £40,000 for charity.

The Fair is always held at the British embassy and it is the one time in the year when that well guarded and sacrosanct place is thrown open to the hoi-polloi of Bangkok, anyone who has the price of an entrance ticket and in the days before its opening, stall holders and their helpers have free access to the grounds.

After the discovery of the body a special meeting was held at which the Fair was reviewed by the ambassador and others in the embassy, as they tried to find some evidence of sinister activity and the ambassador remarked: "It is perfectly probable that the embassy grounds were cased, if that is the right word, during that time."

It seemed to some of the embassy officials that there might have been a plot to plant a body in the lake that would be discovered during the Fair, the purpose being to discredit the embassy. That the plan failed and the body planted in the embassy lake was not discovered until after the fair was, they all thought, probably entirely fortuitous. It was, they believed, pure chance that had caused the body to become wedged under a stone and sink into the mud and weeds that covered the bottom of the lake.

At the Ploenchit Fair this November the sky as always had been hot, blue and cloudless and since early morning the indefatigable committee and their helpers had been busy setting up the numerous stalls, checking the loudspeakers and arranging chairs and tables.

Hundreds of people, Thais and foreigners or farang as they are called, had thronged the great gates of Ploenchit Road and milled around the compound, moving from stall to stall. Cheery voices had commandeered the loudspeakers, beseeching people to roll up, roll up to spend their money; there were games of chance, arts and crafts, special goodies flown in by British Airways, raffle tickets and lots and lots of food to eat. People thronged the stalls selling genuine British fish and chips to be eaten out of genuine British newspapers and the sausages and beer tents were equally popular.

There had been long queues at the food booths and the beer tents had done a brisk trade as usual. Behind the Ambassador's Residence, a small stage and a number of tables had been occupied by the hard drinkers and families with small children. It had been hot and had got hotter by the hour. Groups had picnicked in the shade of the trees waiting for the entertainment to begin. There had been the jazz band from Bobby's Arms, Mr Magic, and some of the local Thai girls crooned their lyrics in to microphones that never left their mouths. The Gurkhas had kept a wary eye on the crowds and security guards had wandered through the stalls collecting money and taking it to the central tally point. There never were any Thai police except for an attachment by the main gate.

Because of the intense heat and the picnic atmosphere most of the visitors wore casual clothes and no one had noticed anyone suspicious wandering through the grounds to the lake behind the house; everyone had been far too busy eating, drinking and having fun.

Mike Horley who ran the hoop-la stall had been determined on this occasion to prevent the highly organised cheating that took place every year when the young participants distracted his attention so that they could place their hoops on the objects of their desire.

The British Council always run a stall selling second hand books at cut prices. The staff running the stall had been kept busy replenishing the books as fast as they ran out and none of them had the time or leisure to notice anything in particular, but when, much later, their memory was jogged, the Director recalled an exchange that could be considered significant.

As the Director recalled it, a Thai man had lounged against the trestle tables, seemingly intent on reading every book as fast as it was put on the table. He had not thought anything of it at the time, a lot of dealers came to the fair to buy the books cheap and then re-sell at a profit.

Then, suddenly, the man had straightened up and held out a book. One of the British Council girls had gone up to him: "You want it?" she had asked him, "It's only 50 Baht."

The man held it up and riffled its pages. In an unnaturally loud voice he had said: "It's a book about sailing I'm looking for."

"That is about sailing", the girl had responded, trying to keep the exasperation from her voice, although she could not help a small moue of irritation at her fellow helpers.

"It is not the one I want", the man replied nonchalantly and he had put the book down with a bang before moving away.

Almost instantly another man, a foreigner this time, had seized the book. "I'll take it", he said and held out a hundred baht note. "Keep the change", he added with a charming smile, "after all, it's all for charity, isn't it?" He had stowed the book carefully away in his bag and moved off in the opposite direction from the Thai man.

Neither the British Council Director nor any of the girls had marked the occurrence as unusual or significant, although everyone concerned longed to be able to dredge up some miracle of memory and so, almost shamefacedly, the episode was recalled during subsequent questions by the police, although no one could see any connection with the body in the lake.

"After all", said Director Jim Dawson, much later, "crime at the Ploenchit Fair? **Drug smuggling?** The mind boggles!"

CHAPTER THREE

The ambassador was holding the weekly meeting. It was held in a room with no outside windows and there was an atmosphere of high security. All the heads of departments were present, as also the director of the British Council, who served as the cultural attache. Usually these meetings served as a forum where everyone could be informed about what was going on, the plans for the future and the implementation of day to day activities. Everyone round the table spoke in turn, summarising the week's doings in his or her department.

The Defence Attache usually opened the proceedings and it was customary for him to tell of meetings with the top Thai military brass, usually conducted on one or other of Bangkok's numerous excellent golf courses. Thai aristocrats and Thai generals (and often they were one and the same) were known for their love of golf.

Then it was the turn of the Consul. Everyone perked up when it was Miss Teresa Blunt's turn, because she had stories to tell of the British prisoners in the Bangkok Hilton as the prison was jocularly called. At any given moment, there were a large number of Brits awaiting trial, usually having been caught with drugs in their possession. Nearly all of them pleaded innocence and some of them had spent many a long year in jail, from where they wrote long letters to the Bangkok Post, to the ambassador and even to the King of Thailand, although it is doubtful if any of those ever reached their destination.

Recently there had been a larger than usual number of letters to the Bangkok Post's letters column known as Postbag, complaining about the difficulty of obtaining British visas for Thai girlfriends and alleged wives. The Postbag is popular with expatriates in Thailand and is extensively used by every farang with a grievance to air, or a solution to the ills of Thailand, from Bangkok's infamous traffic to child prostitution to the politics of golf courses. A perennial favourite, however, was the recalcitrant stance taken by the British embassy to the application by young Thai women for visas enabling them to accompany their British beloveds back home. Once again Teresa Blunt had to defend the procedures and manners of the staff at the visa section.

Today, however, it was Jerry Barton, the head of the drug enforcement police, who had a thrilling story to tell. The Royal Regatta, traditionally held every year in Phuket was approaching, when yachtsmen from all over the world would congregate on this beautiful island. Highly confidential information had been received that a major drug deal was going to go down there during the Regatta and one of the British yachtsmen had been implicated, but possibly falsely, to be used as a decoy. Looking round the table, Jerry said solemnly that the success of the enforcement people, even their safety, depended on absolute confidentiality.

Maurice Pentland Hervey leaned forward and said in his beautifully modulated Oxford accent:

"I am sure that everyone present realises the importance of what we have just heard and I am certain that none of us need reminding that everything that is said in this room is top secret and intended to remain that way."

"Well", said Jim Dawson, the Director of the British Council, "I am afraid all I have to announce is an art exhibition at the Council premises to be opened by Princess Vimolrat and the arrival of a jazz musician who will be performing at the Thailand Cultural Centre next month. He will be featuring some of His Majesty's compositions and we have received a very kind message from the palace which will be included in the brochure."

At this point, a message was brought in to the Ambassador. As soon as he had read it, Mr Pentland Hervey, his face betraying nothing, rose to his feet and asking Jerry Barton to accompany him, left the room. As the meeting had in any case concluded, the rest of them also dispersed.

The Ambassador and Mr Barton made their way to the lake to view the body about which the Admin Officer had just apprised them.

Meanwhile, in a seedy back room of a hotel favoured by backpackers in Bangkok's infamous Khao Sarn Road, another and quite different type of meeting was taking place; the two people in that room were meeting in what was obviously a clandestine manner.

The haven of young tourists who have come to be known (if one is being kind) as budget travellers, the entire area has become a cluster of decrepit looking lodging houses, with names that are supposed to make their 'guests' feel at home, such as Jimmy's Lodge and Cathy's Parlor; others are named after Thai fruits and flowers, Orchid and Apple are much favoured.

Tanned and tousled young people in colourful shorts and tee shirts who look as if they have just come from some sandy beach, amble among the push carts, eating food from the street vendors who line both sides of the road. Everything these backpackers could want is displayed on pushcarts: cheap jewellery, jeans and tee shirts, sandals, beach shorts in psychedelic colours, paperbacks in every European language and even in Hebrew.

No light illumined the guesthouse room and this was

probably just as well for the darkness hid not only the features of the two people, but also the shabbiness and dirt in that room. Something scuttled towards the wardrobe that stood to one side of the bed and one of the two men picked up his shoe and hurled it towards the movement.

"Bloody cockroaches!" he said, "I hate them. Why the hell can't you choose somewhere clean?"

"Like the Sheraton perhaps? Or the Authors Lounge at the Oriental?" the other person jibed. "You know perfectly well that we have to keep out of sight and this is the best place to do that, cockroaches and all."

"When do I leave for Phuket?" Maurice Stone asked. Everything would be more bearable, he felt, if he were within sight of the ocean and Phuket was very beautiful. Marcus recalled his last visit to Phang Nga bay with its picturesque rocks standing up out of the blue-green sea, lined by mangrove swamps.

"Soon, soon", replied the other, "as soon as it is all set up and you know exactly what it is you have to do. You will have your instructions. We must never lose sight of the fact that the drug enforcement chaps are pretty smart and they will be on the watch. They must not know that you have spent time in Bangkok. The first they will see of you will be in Phuket for the King's Cup."

Marcus Stone nodded. His crew members would soon be assembling in Phuket and none of them knew that he was in Bangkok; none of them knew of the trouble he was in. Marcus understood that some time during the race, drugs with a street value of about one million pounds would be placed on board his vessel, his beloved Mark One. Exactly how and when this transfer would take place he was yet to be informed, probably not until after the Regatta began. How the hell had he become involved in this terrible business? Ah well, he knew why and there could be no going back. Somehow they had found and taken possession of a photograph he had not even known existed; it belonged to a long time ago when he had been young and stupid. But if his sponsors were shown that photograph it could spell the end of his sponsorship and his golden days, his image of the perfect young man. The people he was involved with were playing for high stakes and anyone who got in their way would be crushed like some insignificant insect. Marcus Stone had no intention of letting that happen to him and his.

CHAPTER FOUR

When the body found in the lake became general knowledge, there was an atmosphere of gloom in at least two houses on the compound. Sally Martin was married to Third Secretary John and for some time now she had been aware of a coolness in their marital relations. They had been happily married for seven years before arriving in Thailand and it had been quite soon after their arrival that things had begun to change.

Sally attributed what she called John's coldness to the fact that he had fallen in love with someone else. She was well aware of how attractive Thai women were to western men and she had been insecure almost from the day of her arrival in Bangkok.

It was only a few months ago that she had begun to suspect the identity of her husband's lady love. She had reasoned that it had to be someone in the embassy. John did not go out on his own and somehow, she believed that he was not the type to seek casual sex on the streets of Bangkok; for one thing he would be too scared and he was nothing if not cautious. When, one day, she had seen John with Miow at the embassy club she had become convinced that this was John's new love. Even as she had wondered how anyone could be immune to Miow's undeniable attractiveness, she had been filled with an overmastering rage and jealousy. She had watched John flirting with Miow and had seethed with the unfairness of it all. Miow was younger, prettier, had not had two children (or any children, for that matter) and she was obviously exotic...like chocolate cake set beside plain sliced white bread, thought Sally bitterly. That Sally's pale skin did not permit her to lie in the sun and acquire a tan was one of her frustrations and she felt that it made her unattractive to her husband.

Sally had confided some of her anger and jealousy to her friend Patricia, a divorcee who worked in the Commercial Section. Patricia had sought long and hard for a replacement for her husband who had walked out on their marriage after accusing her of trying to emasculate him. She had remained single and always gave the impression that this was a matter of deliberate choice. Patricia was perfectly ready to confirm Sally's belief that men were rats and totally untrustworthy, but that even worse were Thai women who were unscrupulous and anxious for a western husband at any cost.

"Thai men make lousy husbands, unfaithful and they insist on keeping mistresses", Patricia told Sally, with all the experience of two years in Bangkok and no Thai boyfriends, "so they will do anything to get someone like your John."

They both ignored the fact that John stooped, that his hair was receding like an ebb tide leaving nothing in its wake and that he had a very definite tummy bulge from all the duty free booze he put away at the embassy club. Sally looked at John and found him desirable, he was her husband, she loved him and nothing would have convinced her that another woman might not share this opinion.

Now, with the body in the lake and whispers that it might turn out to be Miow who seemed to be mysteriously missing, Sally was in a ferment. She remembered telling Patricia: "I'll kill before I'll let John leave me and the children. I won't take it lying down."

Would the finger of suspicion point at her now? Could Patricia be trusted to hold her tongue and not gossip?

Would people actually believe that she might have murdered Miow Limthongkul? The funny thing was that she knew that she could have done it, she had planned how she might do it hundreds of times; the scenario might vary but it was indubitably a murder story. There were moments when Sally wondered if perhaps she **had** done it and had a sort of black-out afterwards. That was not as unlikely as it sounded for she was prone to blinding migraines and had been known to lose all account of time immediately after an attack. Her migraines had become more frequent since her arrival in Bangkok. Had she killed the Thai girl? She had a vague memory of going to Miow's office to 'have it out with her', as she had expressed it to herself, but she had absolutely no memory of what had taken place after that. Could she have killed her and forgotten it? She was not sure that such things happened outside the thrillers that she loved to read.

Had Miow been in her office when she had gone in there with the intention of having it out? Try as she might, no shred of memory returned to tell her what might have transpired. Had Miow already disappeared or had she been in her office that day? There was no one Sally could ask without it seeming suspicious and Sally knew that quite a few people in the embassy knew of her jealousy, she had never been particularly careful about who might have been listening when she shouted at John.

Now the police were on the compound questioning everybody about their movements and anything they might have seen or heard. What could she tell them when she could not remember the sequence of events herself?

CHAPTER FIVE

At the lake, the gardeners' hosepipe had been requisitioned by the Gurkhas and with looks of utter revulsion on their faces, they obeyed Mr Walcott's instructions to hose the body clean of its enveloping mud.

Tony Walcott stood to one side as they did so, holding his handkerchief to his nose, for the stench was overpowering. He made no attempt to use his mobile phone because he had no earthly idea whom to call and what it was he was about to report. At least, if the body was that of a known person some course of action would suggest itself. Walcott knew that the finding of a body on the embassy compound had, of course, to be reported to the police but not until he had alerted his superiors.

"Oh lord", he moaned silently to himself, "why now, just before the Diplomatic Inspection?" He had been hoping for a quiet chat with John Hamlyn, one of the Inspectors, who was known to be a sort of establishment blue eyed boy, about future prospects.

"Sahib", Ram Bahadur's voice recalled him to the scene and he saw that the Gurkhas had finished washing the mud off and that the body had been laid on its back, staring sightlessly up at the blue sky above. A passing breeze riffled the surface of the lake and he could hear the faraway roar of the traffic, muted by distance.

Clenching his teeth, Tony Walcott strode purposefully up and stared closely at the corpse. Some of its clothing still clung to the body and suggested that it had been clothed in a sarong. The face was unrecognisable; forces other and less benign than the mud at the bottom of the lake, had been at work to ensure that what had once been a human face could not reveal its identity. Tony looked at the Gurkhas questioningly but they shook their heads in vehement denial. Then Ram Bahadur put into words what his superior had already noted: "It is woman, Sahib, body is of female."

"Christ!" Tony exploded, "what the hell is one to do now? Find something to cover it..er..her with but don't move it and not a word about this to anyone. I must go and report this, but remember, no talking."

He turned on his heel and departed for his office leaving the Gurkhas to break into a babble of excited dismay. Eventually, a bedcover was procured and the Gurkhas covered the body with it. As they had been instructed, they left the bedcover and what it concealed by the lake from which it had been retrieved, while they withdrew to go about their duties. There were the gates to be manned and duty rosters to be signed.

The body did not stay there alone for long. Tony Walcott was back with Michael Wilde, the First Secretary who was his immediate boss.

Gingerly, Tony lifted off the bedcover and revealed the body. Wilde shook his head. "Don't know who it can possibly be," he said. "However, something makes me think it is...she is..Thai, not British."

Walcott agreed, it was a conclusion he had already come to.

Michael Wilde continued: "But how the hell did it come to be in our lake?"

Both men turned and regarded the wall which skirted the embassy tennis courts and the Gurkha quarters. On the other side of the wall lay a canal bordered by Soi Somkid, a narrow lane with a few residential high rise buildings.

"Someone could have come over the wall at night with the body. It wouldn't be too difficult for a couple

24

of reasonably fit chaps" said Wilde and again, Tony Walcott agreed. The police would have to question the residents of the soi and discover whether anyone had seen anything. The Gurkhas would certainly have to be questioned; their quarters were close to the wall and they ought to have seen or heard something. The fact that they had not reported any such thing opened them to suspicion.

"Well," he asked, "what do we do now? Inform the police?"

"Yes, but not before we inform HMA. By Jove, he's not going to like this!"

Did anyone? Walcott wondered sardonically, but he held his peace, replaced the bedcover on the corpse and followed his superior back to the office.

CHAPTER SIX

Miow Limthongkul was a very pretty woman, with the sort of figure that attracted attention wherever she went; heads turned and men were always coming on to her. Dressed in jeans and tee shirts or in a slinky dress, such as are to be found on wayside stalls on Sukhumvit Road or at Patpong's night market, it was easy to imagine that she was a bar girl, and for reasons of her own, this was an impression that Miow liked to foster. Everyone called her Miow, which means cat and there was something feline about her tiptilted eyes, her walk and her sinuous ways. Since she kept her remarkable intelligence well hidden, it was easy to dismiss Miow as just another Thai beauty with nothing on her mind beyond making a fast buck and having *sanuk* or a good time. Miow always said that nobody in her life had ever taken her seriously and certainly had never considered her dangerous. "I'm the Thai equivalent of the dumb blonde", she had told Jerry once, "I'm sure I can go like a ghost through all kinds of events and no one would notice me except horny males." And angry wives, she added to herself; how angry that pathetic Sally Martin had been and Miow had been unable to explain to her that she would not look twice at poor old John Martin, one cannot tell a jealous wife that her husband is not desirable.

In fact, Miow was a respected and hard hitting member of the drug enforcement police who worked undercover and she had for a long time been working closely with Jerry Barton at the British embassy, where most people thought she was Barton's secretary.

Educated in England, Miow spoke English as fluently as she did Thai and she knew French and German as well; in fact, she was altogether a most remarkable young woman who seemed equally at home in the seedy dives of Bangkok as she was in its upper class drawing rooms and was well able to tailor her persona to suit any situation in which she might find herself, however unlikely that might be.

It was Miow who had alerted Jerry to the possible involvement of Marcus Stone, the well known British yachtsman in the drug deal that was supposed to take place at Phuket during the world famous Royal Regatta. She had made a number of visits to Phuket in recent weeks and it was during this time that she had stumbled on a lead which pointed directly at the British yachtsman Stone.

It was hard to believe. Marcus Stone was a handsome, wealthy and well educated young man, as far removed from the ugly drug scene as it was possible to be. He had got married quite recently and was the father of a baby boy. There had been many lovely photographs, not only in the yachting magazines, but in all the glossy publications, of Marcus Stone with his beautiful wife Morna and their child, even one of them posing on his yacht the Mark One.

Why would such a man get involved in sordid smuggling? Of course, a man like Stone would have a taste for adventure and danger and smuggling drugs could certainly be said to have both. Somehow, both Jerry and Miow found this hard to swallow, but then as they said, people did all kinds of unlikely things especially when enormous sums of money were involved.

Somehow, Miow felt and Jerry agreed with her, there was more to it than that.

Now, crouched in a small, dingy back room in a part of Krabi that the tourists never see, Miow Limthongkul thought to herself that she had never been in quite such a tight spot before although she had been in many difficult situations.

Nobody in her family knew exactly what Miow did for a living, but her mother suspected that it was probably unsuitable. Miow had a habit of vanishing for days together and then she became unreachable.

"It's all to do with my work," Miow would explain blithely, but her mother could not see why a secretary at the British embassy should need to travel quite as much and as secretively as Miow did. However, she held her peace, for Miow had always done pretty much as she pleased. Besides, Mrs Limthongkul was sure that if she pressed for the truth, it might turn out to be unpalatable. Had she been able to see her daughter now, in hiding, in fear of her life, hunted by an adversary as powerful as Khun Pho, she would not have been able to rest.

Miow had been forced to hide out on Krabi, a picturesque island resort, hidden in a back room by the chef in one of the hotels, whose son had been one of Khun Pho's many victims. It was uncertain how long Miow could safely lie low there. She needed to get a message to Jerry Barton at the embassy, informing him of the narrow escape she had had at the hands of Khun Pho's men and of what was taking place at Phuket. Unfortunately, she had lost her mobile phone and she suspected it had been stolen from her handbag.

She longed to be able to talk to Jerry. Miow had fallen in love with Jerry a long while ago, but she knew that it was unrequited. Although he had never spoken to her of Suzy, Miow had always known that there was someone or something that Jerry could not get over. She hoped that some day he would.

Meanwhile, she concentrated on the problem with which she found herself faced. How was she to get out of Krabi, return to Phuket and from thence to Bangkok?

Her informants had stressed that Khun Pho's men were on the look-out for her and they were desperate which made them doubly dangerous. There was too much riding on Marcus Stone taking possession of the drugs, conservatively estimated at one million pounds, for them to permit her to escape to Bangkok with her knowledge of the deal.

As if in answer to her thoughts Sumet, the chef, came into the room. One look at his face told Miow that he did not have good news.

"I'm sorry", he said, "it is no longer safe for you here. Everybody knows that they are searching for you and one of the waiters, a man I do not trust, saw you last night and he has been asking questions. Khun Pho's men are combing Krabi and it is only a matter of time before they put two and two together. Before that happens I have to get you out."

"I don't want to get you into any trouble Sumet", Miow said, "you have done enough for me already."

"I have an idea", replied Sumet, waving away Miow's words, "it won't be comfortable and I do not know how long you will be safe there, but I thought you might hide in a *horng.*"

A *horng*, as Miow knew, is a room, but in this case she knew that Sumet meant a box canyon. These are accessible at low tide through caves at the base of the limestone outcrops that rise sheer from the Andaman Sea. They are unspoilt, covered in dense greenery from top to bottom, with a few patches of white and reddish clay stained limestone showing through.

"As soon as it gets dark I will take you in a boat to one of the many caves. It is not far from the shrine of Phra Nang".

"Well", said Miow with forced cheerfulness, "the Lady of the Bay should be able to protect me as she does the fishermen."

As soon as the sun set, Sumet was there to lead Miow to the water's edge where a two seat kayak awaited them. A fisherman stood by the boat, ready to hand Miow into it.

Sumet folded his hands together in a *wei* that was both an apology and a farewell. "I do not know the area well so Jham will take you to the *horng*. I have packed some food and water for you and if it becomes necessary, Jham will bring more in a day or two."

Miow smiled at him as cheerfully as she could and thanked him for his kindness. She then stepped into the canoe and was rapidly rowed away.

In the darkness she could discern ageing wooden houses and on the further bank were mangrove forests, thick, dark and sinister in the darkness. The water, usually translucent, with vari-coloured fish swimming over layers of coral, was now dark. There was no moon to cast a silvery light. It was an ideal night for fugitives, thought Miow. She knew that the limestone towering ahead was riddled with caves and that just inside the mouth of one is the shrine to Phra Nang, where both Muslim and Buddhist fishermen leave offerings in hope of a bountiful catch. Houses on stilts sat along the lagoon's edge and Jham explained to her in a whisper that it was a village of fishermen and charcoal makers.

He told her how the red mangrove had to take root quickly before it was swept out to sea by the tide. In the same hoarse whisper, he told her about macaques that swim, of sharks spotted like leopards, of otters and kingfishers and eagles, all of whom competed for fish in the clear and limpid water.

And then the boat slowed as they reached the *horngs*, the caves. Silently and efficiently, Jham beached the boat at the base of the outcroppings.

"All sound is increased here", he warned her and Miow realised that the smallest sound was magnified and reverberated around the sheer canyon walls that framed the sky. She was suddenly aware of a strange clacking noise and instinctively held her breath for a heart stopping moment before Jham explained in a sibilant whisper that it was a crab snapping its claws. Miow almost laughed out loud in relief.

"It's a pity my cell phone is lost," she said. "I don't think you would have been able to use it here," Jham replied, "there would be little or no reception here."

Sumet had packed a small roll of bedding, a little primus stove and various packages filled with food. Jham helped her with her few possessions and then left her to settle down in her new home. As he paddled away, Miow stood and watched the boat dwindling away into the darkness and she felt a cold loneliness possess her soul as she stood there and watched him go and the night enveloped him.

CHAPTER SEVEN

Jerry Barton was silent as he walked to the lake with the ambassador who had divulged the fact that a body had been found in the lake. Neither he nor the ambassador were in the mood for idle chatter. Jerry's mind was a shambles; where was Miow, why had he heard nothing from her and why was he thinking of her now, when this body had been discovered in the lake?

Jerry Barton had once been the pride of his teachers, consistently described as having a fine mind, a person who would go far. Well, he had come as far as Thailand where he worked for the Drug Enforcement Police but he knew that was not what his mentors had in mind. Well, for that matter, it was not what he had planned for himself either. He had expected to go on from Oxford, perhaps into politics, maybe into high finance. However, something had happened while he was at University to change not only his plans, but his whole life as well.

Jerry had fallen in love with Suzy Hawkins. She was reading English Literature at Somerville College. Suzy was very pretty, with long blonde hair that skirted her waist and beautiful blue eyes and she was also extremely bright, her Tutor was sure that she would secure a first at Schools.

Jerry had loved Suzy with all the passion of a man who did not engage in such things lightly. He had a wonderful sense of humour, a charming whimsicality, but essentially he was a very serious person.

Suzy and Jerry were unofficially engaged and intended to marry as soon after their final exams as possible. The final year was fraught for both Suzy and Jerry, both of whom intended to take a First and so both of them were preoccupied and inclined to be jittery.

Jerry never knew exactly when Suzy had begun to change and he was to blame himself bitterly for that, for not seeing the devastation that was beginning to be wrought. At the inquest that was held after Suzy's death, the Coroner's verdict was death by misadventure, for Suzy's body had been found in the Isis, trapped among weeds, with a weeping willow bending down over her. The police report, however, made it plain that she had taken an overdose of drugs and that she had been on drugs for over a year.

Jerry was to ask himself many times over how he could have missed the signs, Suzy's inexplicable changes of mood, her erratic behaviour. How had he let himself be deluded into thinking it was all due to exam fever? He could not forgive himself, for he was sure that had he been more observant he would have saved her life.

In his desperate grief, Jerry spent a lot of time with the police who had investigated Suzy's death. Fortunately, Chief Inspector Morey of the Thames Valley Police was sympathetic and took the time and the trouble to talk and to listen to Jerry. He told him about the stranglehold that drugs could take on an individual's life, changing the personality and how, eventually, it could drive a person to the sort of desperation that had caused Suzy to take her own life.

From that moment, Jerry Barton foreswore everything he had planned and worked for and he sought vengeance in the only way he knew: to fight drugs and that was how he came to be part of the drug enforcement police. He had never forgotten the sight of Suzy's body and although the grief had dimmed, the anger had never left him and was revived every time he encountered the victims of drugs. He brought to his work a sort of crusading passion which, although he was well liked and respected, caused people to feel less than comfortable with him, somehow distanced. Jerry worked closely not only with the Thai police, but also with the American drug enforcement people and with the UN agencies.

Now, as they approached the lake and came within sight of the body lying on its shore, Jerry had a sudden sharp sense of *deja vu*, as he recalled the day Suzy had breen brought up out of the river at Oxford.

After the ambassador and Jerry had viewed the body, the latter called up his friend and associate Inspector Vichai of the Bangkok Metropolitan Police Special Branch. Vichai was a dapper individual who believed above all else in *riep roi*, in orderliness in all things. It had contributed to his success, making him methodical and painstaking. He had cultivated an air of languor which made him seem deceptively easy-going. Vichai had a passion for clothes and was always impeccably turned out in charcoal grey suits cut in the very latest fashion, while his shirts were of almost every colour of the rainbow. It was rumoured that he got all his clothes from bespoke tailors in London.

Inspector Vichai was one of the most respected members of the Homicide team in Bangkok. Thirty six years old, Vichai had a number of successful cases behind him, which had given him a reputation for tenacity, toughness and insight that was sometimes plain brilliant. His enemies might ascribe much of his success to luck, but in fact, Inspector Vichai left nothing to chance, although he had been known to say that he was inclined to meditate on his problems. He was very religious and did a great deal of merit making.

Like so many upper class Thais, Vichai had studied in Britain and later had trained at Scotland Yard and although he himself did not think that he had learned very much that he had not known before, he acknowledged that having been there gave him a sort of edge.

Inspector Vichai regarded Jerry Barton as a very fine policeman but, although unaware of the extent of Barton's personal involvement with drugs, he considered that there was something dangerously fine tuned in the young man, something that might give at any time.

When the call came from the embassy, informing him of the discovery of the body in the lake, Vichai knew at once that Jerry Barton was concealing something: either very great fear or anger. Vichai had an instinct about such things and as he shrugged into his jacket and reknotted his tie, he wondered whose body it was and how it had come to be in the embassy lake. As soon as he arrived at the embassy, he was met by Jerry Barton who looked drawn and distrait. Vichai took one look at him and asked: "You know whose body it is?"

"No", replied Barton, "I wish I did, but it is in a bad state and the face has been mutilated. All we can say at this time is that it is a Thai female in her twenties."

Vichai regarded Jerry carefully. "Where is Miow?" he asked.

An expression of pain crossed Jerry Barton's face and Vichai knew instantly that Barton thought the body might be Miow Limthongkul.

"Miow has been away for some time in Phuket and she has not been in touch", Jerry Barton explained, "I have tried all our usual contacts and everywhere I have drawn a blank so far."

Vichai hesitated, then asked: "You think the body is Miow?"

"Oh Christ, how can I tell?" Jerry burst out, "of course it could be, it's just what the bastards might do if they thought we were getting too close. I warned her but she said she knew what she was doing and besides, it is all part of the job. But I shouldn't have let her go to Phuket by herself without more back-up."

Awkwardly, Vichai patted Barton on the shoulder.

"We shall soon discover whether it is Miow or not. Don't worry", he said tersely, then turned to direct his men to put the corpse into the police van. "I shall be in touch as soon as we know something from Forensic", he said. "Try not to worry", he added, as the van drove away.

Vichai and Barton sat in the latter's office and went over the case together. "Miow had a tip-off that a big deal was going down at Phuket, during the Regatta," Jerry said. "We believe, but have no shred of definite proof, just hearsay from a usually reliable source, that the British yachtsman Marcus Stone is involved and at this end it is more than possible that the elusive Khun Pho could be. With the aerial defoliation of the poppy fields on the Thai-Burma border, he has been forced to look for greener pastures. The drugs have a street value of more than a million pounds. Stone has never before been involved in anything like this and he is independently wealthy. There is also no known connection with Thailand, except through sailing. That could suggest blackmail. Our chaps in Britain have been on the trail but so far they have failed to uncover any evidence of blackmail. That could mean that Stone, for reasons of his own, is playing it close to his chest."

"Why would they murder Miow?" Vichai queried "and why would they put her in the embassy lake?"

"They must have rumbled her, found her connection with us and are giving us a warning to back off."

"If it was meant as a warning, then why deface the corpse?" Vichai asked. "No", he shook his head, "I cannot help thinking that they did that precisely because the body is not Miow's."

"We do not know whether the body was deliberately

36

defaced or whether that happened because of its submersion in the lake," Jerry pointed out.

"No", Vichai agreed, "but we soon will and in any case, I don't think the body was in the lake long enough for that to happen and even if it were, why was only the face mutilated?"

"Good point", responded Jerry and began to look marginally more cheerful, but then his expression changed: "Oh lord, what kind of person would... I wonder who the poor girl was...." he stood up abruptly and turned away to look out of the window.

Vichai regarded his back with sympathy. Jerry took things hard and he felt too deeply. He had not learned detachment which, as a good Buddhist, Vichai had, a quality especially desirable in a policeman. Yet there was no doubting that Barton was an excellent policeman, his police work seemed to feed on and draw sustenance from the passion he felt.

The two men discussed the case exhaustively and then went out to lunch at a nearby noodle stall. Certain members of the embassy who had seen Jerry Barton eating at small wayside restaurants in the company of Thais, had disapproved of this practice, not realising that it was necessary for him to frequent all kinds of places in the line of work; it was fortuitous that such small and unglamorous restaurants also served the most delicious food. This noodle stall was famed for its preparation of chicken, *Khao man kai*, a dish rarely prepared in the home because of its time consuming procedure. Wealthy and fashionable Thais come in droves to eat this chicken.

During lunch, Jerry asked Vichai: "How much money do you think has been circulated through drug trafficking?"

"I'd say roughly Bt 400 to Bt 500 billion is generated by five kinds of illegal businesses each year and that is excluding underground lotteries and contraband smuggling. Drug trafficking, as you and I know, is carried out as organised crime in several border provinces and both local and national politicians are involved. Drug trafficking and money laundering rings cannot survive by themselves, they have to depend on the mechanism and power of the state; that is, they must receive support from police, army and politicians. If they are not politicians themselves, they will support politicians. Then they become *jao phor* or godfathers."

Jerry nodded gloomily. "With Bt 400-500 billion they can buy all the votes they want."

Vichai laughed and it was not a pleasant sound. "Even our prime minister was not above suspicion so one would not be far wrong if one thought *jao phor* were running the country."

Just then the inspector's mobile phone rang. It caused no interest among the other customers as the mobile phone is carried around by almost every second Thai. They are to be seen (and heard) everywhere, holding animated conversations in the most unlikely and noisy locations.

Vichai spoke quietly in Thai and then listened for a long time. When he replaced the phone, his face was grave. He shook his head.

"The news is not good", he said, "the villains have been too clever, they defaced not only the face, but also the fingers so that we cannot match the fingerprints. On the other hand, I would say that this means almost conclusively that it is not Miow, they only want us to think it is."

CHAPTER EIGHT

The news of the body in the lake became known, which it did very promptly, for the Gurkhas spoke about it to the embassy servants and they in their turn, served up the news along with breakfast, to their respective employers.

In every house and flat on the compound nothing else was talked of. Telephones were lifted as people called each other to find out details, discuss the gory find. Little was known because the Gurkhas themselves knew nothing beyond the fact that the body was female and almost certainly Thai, but that did not stop the discussion. Pooky's part in the discovery was made known.

Many of the diplomats were of the opinion that the body had probably been meant to be found on the day of the Ploenchit Fair.

"Imagine!" exclaimed Jenny Palin, "it would have meant total disaster if the body had been found then."

"I think that was what was intended", her husband replied drily, "it was obviously aimed as a warning of some kind."

"What do you mean warning?" demanded Minnie Norris, "who was being warned and what of?"

"Of course I don't know that", replied Palin, "but that seems the most likely explanation. Certainly, it was meant to discredit the embassy as much as possible."

"Oh God, how terrible and I thought one was safe living on the compound", put in Mary Matthews, who was a new arrival in Bangkok and inclined to be very nervous about everything.

"Well, of course you're safe", Jenny Palin said reassuringly, "this is some political thing and has nothing whatever to do with us."

Her husband and John Norris exchanged glances but said nothing. While they were almost certain it had something to do with the drugs scene, there was also the distinct possibility that, if as seemed likely, the body was Miow's someone in the embassy might be involved. Miow had enemies. Both men had heard rumours and besides, the walls in the embassy flats were not very thick, so Sally Martin had been heard many times screaming at her husband that she knew he was in love with Miow, she had been overheard saying that she would kill her. Both men thought it wiser to hold their peace.

It was not only the new arrival Mary Matthews who had to be protected, the news of the discovery had also to be kept from the children and all the nannies were warned not to discuss the find with their charges.

Despite Jenny Palin's comfortable assurances, she and everybody else on the compound had been seriously shaken by the event. It was as if there was nothing that was sacrosanct, as if the security and the immunity of the embassy had been violated. As indeed it had and all the residents on the embassy compound felt not only threatened but also in some way diminished by it. Nothing of this sort had ever occurred before in any country they had been in and they were all appalled by it. Those who tried to dismiss it as being a Thai affair, since the body was definitely not white Anglo-Saxon, nevertheless were disturbed to be living cheek by jowl with crime. That day, in Bangkok, every single member of the British diplomatic corps felt vulnerable in the extreme. It was as uncomfortable a feeling as it was unaccustomed.

Some members of the embassy occupied flats in the condominium on Soi Somkid, the balconies of which looked out over the embassy and its lake. Tom Wright was one of these and when the discovery of the body in the lake became known, he came forward to say that just prior to the Ploenchit Fair, being unable to sleep, he had come out late at night to smoke a cigarette on his balcony. He had become aware of a car behaving rather oddly in the street below but had not been able to see much as it had finally parked just out of sight.

Further questioning of other residents had elicited other sightings of this mysterious car and one of the condominium's security guards had volunteered the information that the car had been parked close to the *klong* just by the embassy's garden gate. At least one of the occupants of the car seemed to have been drunk and in need of support. They had requested him to get a glass of water and when he had come back with it had found only two men, one of whom had drunk the proffered glass of water, saying that the other person was asleep in the car and he had thought no more of it. No one had heard a splash or anything like that, but then with the noise of construction that went on all night, no one could be expected to hear anything much anywhere in Bangkok.

Later, when they returned to ask more questions, the guard agreed that the person he had been told was drunk, for whom he had brought the glass of water, could have been a woman.

It was also significant that the car had concealed the door in the embassy wall used by the gardeners who tended the canna lilies planted outside the wall, the length of the embassy compound. This could mean that one of the Gurkhas was involved; on the other hand, the lock on the door was a flimsy one and any self respecting burglar could pick it with ease or climb over it, for that matter.

At the famous Erawan shrine people gathered, as they

do daily, to make known their dearest wishes, and to offer flowers and food, dancing and music, in return for favours granted. Small birds crammed into cages awaited their release as part of someone's merit making.

The body from the lake lay in the pathology room of the Police Hospital, just opposite. The girl who lay on the steel bed had perhaps never said a prayer to the compassionate Erawan.

The once delicate features of her face were so mutilated that they had collapsed into a featureless mask from which the mud and slime of the lake had been cleaned. The fingers, too, had been defaced so that the fingerprints were unobtainable.

The body had been divested of its clothing and lay on the steel table, defenceless. There is no privacy in violent death. The x-rays that had been taken of its various organs hung attached to light boxes from where their shadows and shapes formed a morbid chiaroscuro

There was the usual background of sounds, running water in the stainless steel sinks and the click of steel instruments clattering against steel trays. The fluorescent lighting and the white tiles and stretchers gave it all an antiseptic look that was deceptive. Nothing was sterile in this place and by normal medical standards it probably was no cleaner than it needed to be to protect the pathologists. The bodies they performed upon were beyond protecting.

The pathologists were now proceeding with the latest DNA tests which would prove conclusively whether or not the body was Miow's. The Y-incision had been made and everything was bared for inspection.

As they worked on the body, Dr Montri reflected, not for the first time, on the finality of death and the utter horror of murder. He could not imagine how any human being could bring himself to kill another creature. For his part, he could not even contemplate killing a chicken! On his birthday, he followed the Thai custom of buying various animals from the slaughter house who were then sent to a farm to live out their reprieve from death in peace. It was a way of making merit and now he wondered at the spiritual fate of those who had killed this girl who lay on the autopsy table. There was complete silence in the room with nothing to be heard but the click of surgical instruments and the hum of the air conditioner.

As they worked silently together, all of them wondered about the identity of the dead girl. Once, just a few short days ago, she had been a living breathing person, unaware of the dreadful fate that awaited her. They had determined that she was quite young, less than twentyfive years of age, that she was small made and judging by her bone structure, had probably been very pretty.

The pathologists' tests would soon prove that she was not Miow, they would be able to piece together her blood type, what she had eaten on the day she was killed, the exact moment of her death and even that she had been dragged and pulled for some way before being dumped in the lake. She had not resisted her killers because she had died ingesting poison which had been administered with her food. They had discovered that the poison had been mixed with a strongly spiced *muu kaeng phet*, spicy pork curry.

They had also discovered that she had been nearly four months pregnant and the foetus had been male, although this was entirely irrelevant. What they had not been able to discover, what was beyond their realm, was the girl's name and identity. They handed over the clues they had garnered from their study of the body to the Special Crime Branch and thereafter, it was entirely a police investigation.

CHAPTER NINE

Inspector Vichai rang up the embassy and spoke to Jerry.

"It is not Miow", he said. He knew that was what Barton would want to hear first. "No," he continued, "we have not yet identified her but we soon will. She had a tattoo on her left hip and my theory is that she is a girl from one of Khun Pho's nightclubs who for some reason had to be eliminated and it was a case of killing two birds with one stone, using her to impersonate Miow."

He could not see Jerry Barton wince. Poor kid, thought Jerry, what a life, what a death. Aloud he said: "No info, I suppose, on Miow's whereabouts?" He tried to keep his voice expressionless but Vichai heard the anxiety.

"No, not exactly, but we are almost definite that she is still on Phuket. Everything points to the fact that she has not left. It is a matter of time only before we locate her." He tried to sound cheerful and optimistic.

"It may only be a matter of time before **they** discover her", Jerry retorted. "I just don't think we have time on our side. It is only a matter of days before the start of the race. Before that they will have to stop Miow from reaching us with the evidence. I have to admit I am very frightened."

Vichai knew only too well that this was true, he too was very much afraid, but he clung to his optimism and reiterated: "I tell you, we will find her before they do. Believe that. I am putting my best people on to it and I myself am leaving for Phuket shortly."

"As a matter of fact, so am I", said Jerry. "The Ambassador is the guest of Bedrock UK who are one of the main sponsors of the Royal Cup and I am going along with him."

Jerry replaced the phone and leaned back in his chair. Marcus Stone was heavily tipped to win the race and if so, the Cup would be presented to him by the ambassador. If, however, he was indeed implicated in the drug deal, as now seemed more than likely, there were going to be major shenanigans. Both Stone and the Thais with whom he was involved would do everything in their power to stop Miow from revealing the truth. What chance did the poor girl have? Jerry covered his face with his hands and groaned aloud. First Suzy and now Miow and he was as helpless today as he had been then. And that poor unknown Thai girl, no one had been able to save her either. Jerry slammed his fist hard against the table and hardly registered the pain. His face looked haunted as his mind went back to those long ago days in Oxford when he and Suzy had been young, innocent and full of hope. Everything had been destroyed then. He would not let that happen again, he would save Miow if it was the last thing he did.

Jerry Barton realised then what he had always known but had not allowed himself to recognise; he loved Miow, had loved her almost from the beginning and now that her life was in jeopardy he knew he could not let her go.

Eventually, patient digging by the police discovered that the Thai man at the British Council's used book stall was one of the right hand men of Khun Pho and that he could not have been there for the fish and chips or the British beer and almost certainly not to indulge his literary tastes. Opinion was divided about the other man, believed to have been a foreigner. It could have been Marcus Stone, although this theory was discounted because the famous British yachtsman would probably have been recognised, or it could have been someone altogether different, merely someone running an errand.

Khun Pho was a Chinese Thai. A legendary figure in Bangkok, it was natural that he spawned many colourful rumours, none of them of the humorous variety. To the American Drug Enforcement Administration, Khun Pho was the epitome of evil, the prince of darkness, the Pablo Escobar of southeast Asia. If, Jerry Barton often said, the unlikely alliance of the governments of Thailand and Burma and western anti-narcotics agencies have their way, this uncrowned king of the Golden Triangle might end up facing the same fate as the Colombian cocaine king gunned down in Medellin. Had they but known it, Khun Pho entertained a savage hatred for American and British alike. The anti-drug campaign financed by the American Drug Enforcement Administration, had begun to seriously affect his business. Aerial defoliation of the poppy fields on Thailand's border with Burma was one of the DEA's measures that was forcing him to look elsewhere for poppy pastures. The establishment of S.P.O.T., the satellite tracker which pinpointed areas where the poppy was being grown and which made sure of its destruction, was the bane of his life.

Pho was inordinately rich and he dressed in white sharkskin suits, wore a quantity of heavy gold jewellery on his person, with a particularly large diamond on his pinky. A young tiger on a lead always lay by his side, a good reason for not approaching too close. He kept a whole menagerie of exotic animals, most of them on the World Wildlife Fund's list of endangered species, but the tiger was his favourite companion. A low and throaty growl from that magnificent creature was warning enough for anyone, although there were many who thought Khun Pho more frightening than his tiger. It was said that every morning Khun Pho drank the juice extracted from a snake and this, it was believed, was the secret of his extraordinary vitality. Nobody knew his exact age, but he was not young and yet he seemed ageless and his prowess with young girls was legendary. This might have been because none of the young girls dared speak the truth....who can tell?

Khun Pho had many ventures, some of them legitimate but all of them concerned with making the maximum possible amount of money. Such is the world that the least legitimate of his many concerns earned the highest rewards. He loved money passionately and it was said that the income generated from the many skin clubs he owned all over Thailand was ninety per cent in cash and that seventy per cent of this was never reported. Tales are told of a locked and sealed room in one of his many mansions which contains nothing but cash. People say that Pho was the victim in his childhood years of such grinding poverty that now nothing but cash and more cash could assuage the pain. Khun Pho was heavily into drugs, not to use but to sell, and it is rumoured that the money generated by this activity surpasses anything the ordinary person can even dream about.

Khun Pho travelled the world first class, surrounded by beautiful young women and he never allowed himself to see the misery of the men and women on whom he battened. He was elusive and difficult to track, but just recently it had been noticed that there were frequent trips to Cambodia by people suspected of being his henchmen. On the day when an agreement was being signed in Phnom Penh providing American aid for narcotics interdiction efforts, customs officials swooped down on a speedboat off the south western province of Koh Khong and seized seventy one kilograms of heroin destined for the west. Among the five smugglers were two policemen who quickly fingered a superior officer as the ringleader. Tipped off, the officer fled but left behind evidence of a connection to Khun Pho. Like most of the evidence uncovered, this connection was almost impossible to prove and yet again Khun Pho was able to evade those who sought to bring him to justice and to end his reign of terror.

Of course, when the body in the lake was discovered, it was not immediately connected with Khun Pho and his underworld.

At his headquarters in Yaowarat (Chinatown), an innocuous looking building in a narrow, congested soi, Khun Pho leaned back in his massive carved chair, inlaid with the ivory of some hapless elephant and regarded his henchmen. They were nicknamed Lek and Nok because the first was very small and the second had the look of an unfledged bird.

"So", he said, "the girl managed to evade you." His voice was soft and silky, but the menace was unmistakable. Everyone knew that the more softly he spoke, the greater was his rage.

Lek and Nok fidgeted uneasily and shifted on their feet. "But," Nok protested, "that is the plan. She thinks we are after her and she hides. Out of sight and out of action." The sheer brilliance of this caused him to giggle a little.

"We will find her when we need her, never fear", said Lek with false heartiness, "after everything is over and then she will tumble like a fish into our net. We return to Phuket tonight, meanwhile we have men who know every inch of that place searching for her and that will be the end of her."

"Indeed? And do you have the faintest idea where she might be?" Pho's voice rippled like silk.

"We will comb Phuket; if she is not there, she will

be on a nearby island and we will trap her there. It is certain she has not reached the embassy in Bangkok, that means she is still somewhere on the island and the men searching for her are fishermen from that place. They know every bit of it like the palm of their hand," said Nok.

"And what of the brilliant plan of the body in the lake, have they worked it out yet?"

Again both Nok and Lek fidgeted, for from their master's voice they could not tell whether he meant what he said or not. Khun Pho could be savagely sarcastic. They exchanged glances and then Lek spoke: "It has been found and Jelly Barton thinks it is Miow. That will teach those farang not to interfere with us. It would have been Miow if we had been able to catch her in time and had it been found as we intended at the Ploenchit Fair it would have shut the embassy up completely. It was a warning and they will not be able to find out the identity of the body for we have defaced her and removed the fingerprints."

"Well, that at least was clever", Khun Pho conceded, "but as that plan failed we now have to reckon that Barton will soon be on our trail...unless that girl is stopped." He looked at his two henchmen who were twisting and turning, cracking their knuckles and shifting from foot to foot. Then he smiled. "It's all right boys, you have done a good job. Keep the little bitch out of sight cowering with fear and out of the way until it's all over and then you can dispose of her. Well done."

It did not occur to either of them to be surprised that Khun Pho never asked the identity of the dead girl. She was unimportant, insignificant and she had been expended. Her only reason for dying was a superficial resemblance to Miow Limthongkul and the fact that girls like her were entirely expendable, no questions asked. Nok and Lek had decided after everything was over, to send some money to her parents in their Isaan village and they would do some other merit making, perhaps release a few caged birds or save some cows from slaughter, that would take care of it.

"Has Stone arrived in Phuket?"

"Yes sir, he is there now."

"I trust he has been well briefed and knows exactly what is expected of him," said Khun Pho.

"He knows", replied Lek, while Nok, grinning evilly, mimed a throat being slit.

Khun Pho dismissed them with a careless wave of his hand. He had other and more important things to occupy him.

He knew that his henchmen had been unable to understand why he had selected Marcus Stone to be his courier. They knew that Marcus was unwilling, had been blackmailed into agreement and as far as they were concerned, was more trouble than he was worth. There were a great many people who were only too willing to act as couriers for Khun Pho. Drug smuggling was so profitable that people forgot about the danger, going readily into countries such as Singapore and Vietnam where, if caught, it meant death by execution.

What they did not know was how much Pho hated the British. No one knew exactly why or how it had all begun and he was not about to enlighten them. He was determined that this time he would bring down Marcus Stone (the darling of the yachting world), although he neither knew nor cared anything for man and with him the British embassy, the emblem of his hatred, would be brought low

CHAPTER TEN

Phuket was preparing for the annual Regatta. Ten years after the first Phuket King's Cup Regatta, the Commodore Dr Rachot Kanjanavanit is proud of what has been achieved. Phuket, he had always known, had the ideal conditions for sailing and the Yacht Club was an ideal base for a regatta.

The Ninth King's Cup Regatta has a special significance because it represents an auspicious conjunction of nines: the ninth Regatta dedicated as always to King Bhumiphol Adulyadej, who is the ninth Rama of the ruling Chakri dynasty and acceded to the throne on the ninth of June. The King was himself an accomplished sailor who took a great deal of interest in the event, as he did also in so many other areas such as music.

The boats had begun gathering at Phuket: cruisers, lasers, and catamarans. There was bustle and activity as people worked on their boats readying them for the start of the race. They carried all kinds of names, representing the dreams and fantasies of their owners: Sweet Swan, LastTango, Cat lady, Ultima Thule.

The ninth Regatta, like all its predecessors, is not just a series of races with a lot of yachties standing about drinking beer and holding post mortems. There was a lot of fun to be had, beginning with a party on the first Saturday of the Regatta at the Boat Lagoon. Although the skies opened and an unforeseen storm raged from the north east and lashed into the Boat Lagoon, nobody allowed it to spoil their fun. The fearless sailors crowded inside where, sheltered from the stormy blast, they listened while a Thai band played on the foredeck of a yacht and never missed a note in the 35 knot driving rain! Equally undaunted, a bevy of lovely Thai ladies armed with huge umbrellas battled the fierce head wind while they retrieved case after case of ice cold Singha beer from the stall up wind of the party and sprinted back to serve the yachtsmen huddled against the walls.

Marcus Stone was one of that number and he stood there gloomily nursing a beer, wondering when and how the drop was going to be made. Once he took possession of the drugs he knew that he would be in mortal danger. He looked cautiously around him wondering if there were any under cover drug enforcement people in the crowd. There were almost certain to be, there was no way such a big deal could go down without someone being tipped off.

People were laughing and joking all around him and he heard them speculating whether the unforeseen rain was a good or bad omen. Stone had never been much for omens and other superstitions but now he listened and was strangely pleased when one man, a Thai who claimed to know such things, declared categorically that it was a splendid omen. But it did little to lighten his mood and he stood there while happy laughing and inebriated people eddied and flowed around him like so much flotsam and jetsam. Belatedly, it occurred to him that the rain could be a good omen for the police and not for him.

Excitement was rife. The Big Eagle, a Humphreys 50, had narrowly missed winning last year and now was heavily favoured. The owner, Will Masson, had refitted The Big Eagle with a larger propeller, a new jib and even super new air conditioning.

However, there were plenty of other boats that had also been specially refurbished for the big event. Australia's Jay Robinson had a top crew with him on Millennia and everyone knew he was intent on winning and was also already in training for the America's Cup.

Ultima Thule, a Schumaker 50 from the States was a strong contender for the Phi Phi to Nai Harn race. The Brunei based Fantasy was said to be using a much smaller mainsail and no extendable bowsprit which means a lot more off the wind boat speed.

Miow had thought she would be unable to sleep that night in her lonely hideaway but, in fact, lulled by the sound of the sea she had slept long and dreamlessly. The cave ledge where she had set up house was dry and snug despite a pervasive smell of fish and seaweed. When, as now, the tide came in, water swirled around in the cave beneath her. Blessing Sumet, Miow lit the primus stove and opened packages to make a breakfast of chicken, boiled eggs and tea.

Later, as the tide receded, she went down into the caves and looked around her at the sheer canyon walls that framed the sky. She knew that some of these caves had been inhabited by prehistoric men some 50,000 years ago and she had heard that stone tools, beads and human relics were still being discovered. She smiled grimly to herself and hoped that hers would not be among them.

Boats went by at infrequent intervals and she knew that most of them carried tourists, paddling past the massive rock walls behind which she hid herself. They were intent, she knew, on watching the schools of many coloured fish that swarmed away from the boats. Kingfishers with their bright plumage of blue and scarlet and yellow, wheeled among the rock canyons, while a troop of monkeys scampered among the trees growing out of the cliff face.

It was a beautiful morning of blue and gold and it depressed Miow unutterably that she had to hide here in the dark shadow of the cave unable to do anything but wait. And if Khun Pho's men had picked up her trail she could hope for no reprieve; they would kill her with no more thought than a fisherman has when he guts the fish he has caught.

Miow knew, none better, that a great deal was at stake in the struggle for control of southeast Asia's booming opium trade. Burma had, for the sixth consecutive year, produced yet another bumper crop of more than 2000 tonnes of raw opium, up from the 500 to 600 tonnes produced in the eighties. It takes about 10 kilos of opium to produce one kilo of heroin and Miow could reel off the figures: that one kilo was worth $10000 in Bangkok and twenty times that on the streets of London or New York, making the trade worth hundreds of millions of dollars. Worth fighting for, definitely worth protecting at all costs and she knew that was what Khun Pho would do.

She had to wait until it was dark and the tide was right before she could expect Jham to come with news, more supplies and she had to admit to herself, even more important, was the sight of a friendly human face. Miow felt very desolate indeed.

What was Jerry doing, she wondered? Had he already realised that she was in trouble? Of course, she reminded herself, he must know something was wrong since he had heard nothing from her or of her. He would come looking for her, she was sure of that, but they were running out of time. The Ninth Regatta was due to start and she had to be there, on the spot to try and stop it. No one knew how and where or when exactly the drop was to be made. She had to find that out and that information had to be conveyed quickly to Jerry, but how was she to do it stuck in this cave with Khun Pho's men closing in on her?

Miow would say later that she did not know exactly how or when it struck her, but suddenly she knew that she had been tricked into hiding in the caves. Her pursuers had let it be known that they were looking for her and she had unwittingly fallen in with their plan. It was obvious to her now: of course they wanted her out of the way. Oh God, how was she ever going to get to the regatta in time marooned as she was?

At the British embassy, it had become generally known that the body in the lake was not Miow. Everyone was glad of that and some of them spared a thought for the poor young victim. They speculated avidly about who she might be but they were relieved that, as far as anyone could tell, she had no connection with the embassy. "Not even one of the maids", they told each other, "and none of the domestics seem to claim her as family".

Sally Martin broke into hysterical tears when Patricia told her jokingly: "Well, turns out it isn't our little Miss Cat. Bet you wished it was!" She was entirely unaware of Sally's torment, of her fear that she had done something terrible that she could not remember. Her friend stared at her, horrified. "Steady, old girl, what's the matter with you? I was only joking. It's some unknown Thai girl whose body was found, poor kid, but there's nothing for you to get so upset about."

'If only she knew', thought Sally to herself and said a quiet prayer for the poor dead girl. If everybody knew that the body was not Miow then there could be no shadow of suspicion pointing her way. They said that, so far, they had been unable to find any connection between the victim and anybody at the embassy.

It was over, the dreadful feeling of being capable of murder, Sally was back to normal and she told herself that she would never travel down that dark and lonely road again. She determined that she would have it out with John that very evening and settle the matter once and for all. Actually, she knew now and it was like having a veil removed and being able to see clearly, that John loved her and the children. He might admire Miow Limthongkul (which man did not?) but she felt certain now that there was nothing more to it than that.

When John returned from work that day, he found his wife dressed prettily, waiting for him with a drink ready. She had been a bit off lately, he had thought, giving him the silent treatment and so he eyed her warily. He waited for her to speak first for he was sure that something was brewing and he only hoped it wasn't another spate of unpleasantness.

"You heard I suppose", she said, "about the identity of the girl in the lake?"

"Oh yes," he replied, "poor kid. One is happy it isn't Miow, but it's a bloody shame about that poor girl whoever she is."

Those did not sound like the words of a man in love, but Sally probed further. "What do you think has happened to Miow?" she asked.

John looked at her warily, thinking, here it comes; the old girl had some funny notion that he was in love with Miow, had been accusing him on and off for months. Of course he thought Miow attractive, any normal man would, but he was not and never had been in love with her. Wouldn't have been much good if he were because he knew Miow was in love with Jerry Barton. Carefully, he replied: "I haven't the faintest but I do know she can take care of herself and anyway, she has Jerry Barton looking out for her. Sal, old girl, I'm starving, what's for dinner?"

CHAPTER ELEVEN

Everyone gathered to study the racing schedule. The Regatta opened on Sunday December 3 with the BMW Race for Catamarans from Nai Harn Bay. Monday was Ballantine's Race towards Phi Phi Island and so on until Friday December 8.

Most of the western competitors in the Ninth Regatta knew each other from other races such as the Whitbread, the Kendal Cup and the Mumm Champagne, besides the four big south east Asia regattas, so there was a great deal of camaraderie. Only Marcus Stone stayed aloof from all the bustle and chatter around him. Nobody really noticed because, although not unfriendly, Marcus had never been among the most convivial of the sailors. If they thought about it at all, they put it down to his British reserve. So no one there guessed that Marcus, the darling of the media, the perfect success story, was just plain terrified.

In his room, Marcus had put out photographs of his wife Morna and their baby son. He picked up the silver framed picture of his wife and muttered: "You know I have to do this darling, but pray God it will all come right."

He would be given the precious, the damnable cargo, to be stowed away on his beloved Mark One on the second last day of the Regatta. To avoid any possible suspicion, in case someone had been watching them, the person who would hand over the drugs would be someone Marcus had never seen before. It had all been carefully explained to him during the meeting at Khao Sarn Road by that mysterious person whose nationality, like everything else about him, had been shrouded in mystery.

Marcus went over the whole damned business for

the umpteenth time; his mind was like a hamster on a treadmill unable to get off it, as he played and replayed the sequence of events. He could not wish that his son had never been born and if he had not, perhaps it would have been Morna they would have threatened... equally unthinkable. He had given hostages to fortune and the time had come to pay the ransom. These mysterious and terrible people had, it seemed, covered all the bets.

Despite everything that had taken place, the embassy had to go on as if nothing had occurred. "At least", they said to one another, "we should be grateful the body wasn't discovered during the Ploenchit Fair, we would never have been able to keep things under wraps then and it would all have been plastered over the front pages of the Bangkok Post." And they shuddered at the thought of the publicity averted.

One of the events that had to go on was the Christmas Pantomime.

"Everyone looks forward to that", said Shirley Mason, the Ambassador's secretary, almost in extenuation and they all agreed with her. They would have been surprised to learn that the natives of many countries where they had performed, had never understood the British *penchant* for cross dressing and scatological humour which characterizes most pantomimes.

This year's panto was to be Cinderella and the script had already been written and approved; it had some lovely opportunities for risque humour centred on the Stepmother and the Ugly Sisters, but it was expected that Michael Wilde would turn in his usual splendid performance as the Fairy Godmother, where fairy was understood not to be a creature of the spirit world, a performance unlikely to please any genuinely gay person.

The embassy, depressed by the murder in their midst, the belief that the body in the lake had been placed there to humiliate the embassy and the constant police presence that had resulted, felt that they were more than entitled to the simple pleasures of Cinderella.

"A good laugh, that's what we all need", said Jenny Palin and everyone agreed. Nobody referred to the fact that Jerry Barton and Miow had both agreed to take part. Jerry was going around like a thundercloud and Miow.... well, nobody knew what had happened to Miow.

Miow, having realised that she had been tricked into hiding, knew that she could not wait for Jham's next visit when he would bring her food and drink. There was no time to be lost, god only knew if she was already too late, but she had to make her way back to Phuket and the regatta. How was she to do it? Looking out across the water, she could see sails in the distance. Quickly she began to light a fire and taking off her tee shirt she draped it on a piece of driftwood and began to wave it furiously. The boat came nearer but no one seemed to be paying any attention to her signals. There was only one thing for it and without giving herself time for reflection Miow divested herself of her clothes and slipping into the water, she struck out towards the boat. She was a good swimmer, although unprepared for the coldness of the water as it closed around her almost unclothed body. She struck out strongly for the boat she had seen but soon realised that it was further away than she had imagined when she saw it from the mouth of the *horng*. She tried not to panic and closed her mind to the possibility that her strength might give out before she either reached the boat or was noticed by its passengers. She just had to go on and she slowed to an easy crawl, trying to rest while she trod water, but soon realised that this was only increasing the distance between her and the boat. Raising her head she gave one despairing shout and then began swimming furiously again. How useless it would all be if she just drowned here, achieving nothing. How tragic too, that she would never see Jerry again and he would never know how she felt about him.

Her strength was giving out so she turned on her back and allowed herself to float, shutting her eyes to the sun's hot gaze. Irrelevantly she thought, 'I shall be burned black' and gave a laugh that turned into a small sob as she realised that the colour of her skin wouldn't matter if she was dead.

Just then she felt hands closing on her and briefly, unconsciously, she struggled to get free. "Take it easy now", said a voice that was unmistakably American, "you are safe. Just hang on and I'll get you on board in no time at all."

"Oh thank God!" she managed to gasp as her saviour began to tow her away.

"Yep," he answered, "you can thank God and me when we get there."

Miow managed to smile before she fainted.

When she came to, she was being hauled on to the deck of a yacht and she heard her rescuer say: "Oh, she speaks English but what the hell she was doing there, your guess is as good as mine."

Miow opened her eyes and looked up at what looked like a lot of legs. Her gaze travelled upwards and she saw the faces they belonged to. There were about four or five people, men and women, and she was glad to see that they were all foreigners, it would have been too embarrassing had they been Thai.

She realised that she was a strange sight in her bra and panties and obviously they did too, or perhaps it was because her teeth were chattering, but one of the women brought a large towel and wrapped it about her. As she did so, she asked: "What happened, honey?"

How was Miow to answer this kindly and perfectly natural question. She felt unable to make up a quick and convincing answer, she could not tell them the truth and yet she was loth to tell them a lie.

"You must forgive me", she said, "I cannot tell you anything at this time but I hope you will trust me and take me to Phuket."

The Americans looked at one another and there was a quick consultation among them which was inaudible to Miow.

"Well", said the man who had rescued her, "I guess it's your secret and you don't have to share it with us, but heck, we're all dying of curiosity."

Miow laughed weakly. "I guess you are", she answered, "but it's not really my secret. When its all over, if you are still around, I'll be happy to tell you."

She was feeling stronger as she sat up and sipped the hot strong coffee that one of the women had brought her. She munched a cookie and looked at the tanned and healthy faces that surrounded her, gazing at her with uninhibited interest.

"Hey! Where are our manners?" the speaker was the younger of the two men, "the gals are Janet, Sara and Judy. I'm Greg and your rescuer there is Tony. Lucky for you he was scuba diving and caught sight of you floating among the fish."

"I'm Sukanya but everyone calls me Miow."

"Which means cat and everyone knows that animal doesn't like water", said Tony meaningly.

Miow recognised the trace of irritation in his voice, knew that he expected to be told, that having rescued her, he felt she somehow owed him an explanation, as indeed, she did.

"If you are still around after the Regatta, I promise I

will tell you the whole story. Please trust me," she repeated.

"We shall certainly be around, I surely will, for I live here," Tony replied.

"Then it's a date", said Miow with her most winning smile.

They turned the boat around and made for Patong beach. Sara, who was the closest in size, furnished a pair of shorts and a tee shirt for Miow and she was glad to be able to divest herself of her wet underclothes.

As she turned to go, Tony came up behind her. "I still want to hear the whole story, remember, so I shall be looking for you."

Was there some undercurrent in his words? Miow looked into his eyes and saw nothing but her own reflection. She shook herself impatiently, telling herself not to be paranoid, even as she smiled and said: "I promise, just as soon as I can".

CHAPTER TWELVE

Jerry Barton and the British Ambassador Maurice Pentland Hervey travelled to Phuket by the early morning plane. They breakfasted on the plane, speaking little. Both men were tense and weary of the tension they had been enduring ever since the body had been discovered in the embassy lake.

"What exactly is our plan of action when we get there?" the ambassador asked, as the trays were removed by a smiling hostess.

"For you, business as usual", replied Jerry. "There must be no indication that anything is amiss. I have to try and find Miow and shadow Stone. He seems to have given Miow and her chaps the slip on a number of occasions."

The ambassador turned in his seat to look at Jerry. He was uncomfortable but felt it was his duty to ask the question that had been troubling him for some time.

"Is she entirely reliable?" he asked tentatively, "I mean to say....."

The words petered out as Jerry turned to him with a bleak expression. "I would stake my life on her reliability, what I fear is that she has staked hers."

"You don't think that..." again, the words died.

"I don't know what to think. I pray not."

Jerry Barton, like Miow, had been thinking things through and it had occurred to him that the information they had so conveniently received about the possible involvement of Marcus Stone was probably a blind. It just did not make sense to use such a highly public figure to smuggle drugs; he certainly did not need the money, although of course, there was no accounting for people's greed. Of course, there was always the possibility of blackmail. Everyone has some secret they would prefer not to have dredged up, but would he go to such incredible lengths?

So what was the motive? Someone trying to discredit Stone? It was possible but not very probable. And what about the body of the girl in the embassy lake, what was the purpose of that? Jerry had begun to think that someone was out to get the British embassy. After all, had the body been discovered during the Ploenchit Fair (as now seemed more than likely), it would have caused a major scandal. Her majesty Queen Elizabeth was due to visit Thailand on a state visit and the embarrassment that would have been caused at the fair would probably have ruined the visit, perhaps have ensured that it would never take place.

So who was behind this enormous effort that had caused Miow to disappear and now was bringing him to Phuket to watch an internationally renowned yachtsman who might be a drug smuggler? He had no answer for that.

As if in response to his thought, the ambassador asked: "Jerry, do we really have nothing tangible to go on? And if Marcus Stone is a smuggler how in hell are we going to cope with that?"

Jerry shook his head. "We've just got to pray for a break through, some sort of bloody miracle. I don't think, however, that Stone is a smuggler, but I don't know anything for sure."

The ambassador put his face in his hands and groaned softly.

"Why this, why me?"

Jerry knew that Pentland Hervey, too, was thinking of the scandal and of the Queen's impending visit and it was only human for him to think of the knighthood he would receive if all went well for her visit. What would he receive if everything blew up in their face: the body in the embassy lake, the involvement of a world famous

British yachtsman? It was too awful even to contemplate.

The hostess was announcing in her fractured English that the plane was preparing to descend and as they obediently straightened their seats and fastened belts, no more was said. The hostess thanked her passengers for flying the 'loyal orchid service' and Maurice Pentland Hervey and Jerry Barton disembarked with wan smiles, neither of them relishing what lay ahead.

At the yacht club, they were in the thick of the races. People and boats were coming and going all the time and there was an air of excitement.

Marcus Stone was preparing for his big race, but all the time he talked with his crew, worked out their strategy, studied the currents and tide tables, his mind kept going back to the message he had received last night.

A young Thai woman had slipped into his room. She had used a key so he assumed she was on the staff of the hotel.

"What do you want, what are you doing here?" he had demanded, his voice rough with the tension he had been under.

"Lelax", she replied gently, "I do no harm, bring you message."

"Well?" Stone demanded, when she seemed to pause, "what is it?"

"It is tomollow", she whispered, unable like most Thais to pronounce the letter r, coming closer to him and he smelt her cheap perfume which could not obliterate the ubiquitous smell of fish sauce and garlic. "Tomollow you will leceive it before you are sail in Ballantine lace. You must get out of sight of the Committee boat and all other boats between Koh

Dokmai and Koh Kai." She unrolled a small map and showed him the two small atolls she had named. She pointed to another rocky outcrop named Hin Mu Sang which was off the main course. "Here", she said, tapping it with her finger.

Marcus noticed irrelevantly that her fingers were long and shapely with polished fingernails.

"But", he protested, "that's impossible, I will be seen!"

"You are the best", she smiled, was she teasing him? "You will manage ok." She laughed and looking back at him over her shoulder with the natural coquettishness of Thai women, was gone as silently as she had come.

Marcus had spent a long time alone after that deep in thought.

He had thought back to the time when he had first been contacted. His instinct then had been to say: 'Go ahead, do your damnedest and see if I care.' But then he had looked at his wife and their beautiful baby son and he had second thoughts. These were ruthless people he was dealing with, he had realised that from the beginning, but if it were only he that was involved he would have told them to go to hell. So they had an incriminating picture of him from way back when, so his sponsors were homophobes and would almost certainly have withdrawn all sponsorship, yet he would have survived. But he had been unable to risk Morna's and their little son's lives and the wretches had made doubly sure by threatening their safety.

Now Marcus stood there in the club and knew that his mind was made up. It would not matter if he never sailed again. It was over.

CHAPTER THIRTEEN

At the police station, Pol cap Manote slowly lowered the telephone receiver. He stared straight in front of him. Never in all his career had he faced anything like this. There had been the occasional theft, a stabbing or two and the odd pocket picked, but nothing of this gravity and he was unsure what to do.

Manote's grasp of the English language was rudimentary. His sparse contact with foreign tourists on Phuket had been limited to sentences of extreme brevity, usually consisting of no more than a word or two. So how was he expected to deal with the information he had just received on the telephone? According to that information a well known sailor competing in the King's Cup race was involved in smuggling drugs and he had been told that if he took a small boat and reached Hu Min Sang he would be able to apprehend the smuggler redhanded.

Pol cap Manote was not at all keen on this suggestion. Smugglers, from his sketchy knowledge of them, were apt to be violent characters who would stop at nothing to make sure of their rewards and usually they had behind them some very influential persons. And apparently, this particular bit of drugs was worth millions of baht. He was not paid enough to undertake such dangerous work and get between the smuggler and his money, none of which would find its way into **his** pocket, that would have put a different complexion on the matter.

On the other hand, if he followed his instinct and sat tight and was discovered doing so, he could get into serious shit. The government was making all kinds of threatening noises about drugs and smuggling and if it was found later that he had simply kept quiet he might well lose his job or be moved to a really active post and that would not suit him at all. Manote decided to do what he usually did, after all, who better to catch criminals than other criminals? His mind immediately went to Khun Lek and Khun Nok, both well known to him and the source of generous handouts in the past and undoubtedly pastmasters of criminality. In fact, he was sure he had recognised Khun Lek's voice on the telephone which was one of the reasons to enlist their help.

He promptly set about telephoning Khun Lek and as they spoke Manote silently congratulated himself on his perspicacity; there was no doubt that his earlier caller with the obviously disguised voice was none other than Lek. Nevertheless, he went through the charade of describing the call and asked for help.

"Oh no," replied Lek, "I am busy with other things and cannot go with you." He did not add that there was no way he could afford to be seen by Marcus Stone. "Tell you what, as a special favour to you I will send you someone. He's much bigger and stronger than you or me and just the sight of him will strike terror into your smugglers."

The Pol cap had, perforce, to be satisfied with that although he would have vastly preferred to leave the entire matter in the capable hands of the burly individual described by Lek.

Having made his decision, Marcus Stone felt at peace with himself for the first time in a long while. He had put through two calls to the UK and was well satisfied with both. He had told Morna to call the police to ask for protection for herself and their baby son. Then he had called his sponsors. He had explained the whole situation to them and they had been appalled. However, they had agreed to let the matter ride for the moment while they thought things over. The idea of any scandal was naturally repugnant to them but they were prepared to take into account the fact that Stone's misdemeanour had taken place a very long time ago and that he was now a happily married husband and father who was ready to go to any lengths to protect his family.

It might mean new beginnings for him but Marcus was full of optimism. He was, at last, his own man again. That was when the thought came to him and he went once more to the telephone.

The embassy informed him that Jerry Barton and the Ambassador had both left for Phuket. Marcus Stone then made his fourth call after which he set out for the Yacht Club.

The King's Cup is sailed under the Channel Handicap System (CHS) a yardstick measure that handicaps all types of yachts. The race, therefore, tends to depend greatly on the weather conditions of the day and how they favour one yacht over another. There were ocean multi-hulls like Flying Colours, Aussie Sheila, a J-130 off the wind flyer called Panorama, and in the cruising class the Alpha Plus were definitely ones to watch out for. The King's Cup is a race with its own history, its very own mythology and its legendary heroes.

After the rain of the night before, the sea was calm and sapphire blue but there was a good wind blowing. One year, Stone remembered hearing, a champagne company sponsor gave the winners a man's weight in champagne. "Pity it's not on offer this year", laughed Simon Brent, his crew member, "You must be 136 kg and on average, by my reckoning, that would equal about 14 dozen bottles!"

Marcus laughed too. He would have laughed at anything just then, life was good again. And he was going to win the race as well, he felt lucky.

Miow would have been surprised had she been able to see what her rescuers were up to after they had deposited her on Patong. After the women who served as protective colour for them had been deposited at their hotel, the man called Tony said tersely to Greg: "That's the girl Pho's men are supposed to be keeping under wraps! How the hell did she find her way in to the sea and what is she up to?"

"Why did you let her go?" Greg replied, "shouldn't we at least keep tabs on her? I wouldn't mind keeping my eye on her, she's a tasty dish."

"You'll be better off if you keep your mind on the job", snapped Tony, "Pho doesn't suffer fools and there can be no mistakes."

"Well, what are we going to do then?" asked Greg.

"First off, we inform Lek and Nok that their bird has flown. Meanwhile, we get on with our part of the job. The pick up has to be made at precisely the moment that Stone thinks he is making the pick up, then while he really gets picked up by the police we sail off to our reward." He laughed nastily. "After it's all over, I wouldn't mind picking up Miss Cat and seeing if she's half as good as she looks." His laugh was chilling.

Greg said nothing; he knew that Tony was not in a good mood and he had long ago learned to steer clear of his partner when he was like that. They had met in Bali while Greg had been on holiday there, when he was down on his luck, desperate to remain on the beautiful island, but rapidly running out of money. Tony had given him his first assignment then and he had made more money than he could ever have imagined. The entire operation had gone smoothly but it had given him a rush that he had enjoyed. Nevertheless, he had wanted out, a return to his peacefully idle existence and had discovered then that he was enmeshed, that there was no possibility of getting out, not until his employers were willing to let him go. Well, thought Greg, the rewards were good and he enjoyed the danger, the rush of adrenalin which, he had discovered, was as addictive in its way as the drugs were to his victims. Sometimes, he thought of his simple parents living in midwestern America who had no idea what their youngest son was really doing. They wrote to him *poste restante* urging him to return to the States while to their neighbours they spoke with pride of their son working as an oilman in the far east. Greg thought with nostalgia of his childhood sweetheart Mary Ellen and of the innocence of his life with her but he knew there was no going back. Not immediately, anyway.

He also knew that if he was caught in Thailand it would mean life imprisonment and in most of the other countries of the region he would probably hang. The Drug Enforcement Agency of the US was coming down hard in the Golden Triangle and President Clinton in his speech to the UN had announced that the US was identifying and putting on notice those countries that tolerate the laundering of drug money and had threatened economic sanctions against governments that failed to crack down on the drug trade. Thailand had responded by tightening surveillance because it had no wish to end up on the list of countries "decertified" by America which would give it virtual outlaw status such as that of Burma, Afghanistan, Iran, Syria and Nigeria. This had made the whole operation more dangerous and the risks were as high as the rewards.

It was well known that Khun Pho had showered many high ranking people with lavish gifts and kickbacks but Khun Pho would protect people like Tony and Greg only in so far as he was protecting his investment and no further. They, Tony and he, were on their own but Greg tried not to dwell on this aspect of the business, just as he tried never to think about the people who were enslaved by the drugs he smuggled, whose lives were all too often ruined by their addiction.

"Well, what's the next step?" he asked Tony. "Do you think your Miss Cat suspected anything? Why do you suppose she was in the water just there?"

"No, I think she was hiding out somewhere from our friends Lek and Nok and for some reason decided to make a run for it. That's just what I was trying to discover but she was too coy for me. We have to find out exactly when our fall guy Stone is going to make his pick-up and get ready to go when he does. The DEA guys are in Phuket and Barton of the British embassy is coming in as well, pretending to be a sailing enthusiast. While they all train their guns on Stone, we get out with the goods."

"Lek will get in touch, that's what he said", said Greg. The presence of the Drug Enforcement Agency suggested what Tony had suspected for some time: that they were on to something. Which was why this elaborate bluff using Stone had been set up, although Pho might have his own secret agenda as well. With that guy, as both Tony and Greg knew only too well, there was never any telling.

Meanwhile, the job had to be done. As soon as they received word from Lek they would have to move.

CHAPTER FOURTEEN

Having escorted the ambassador to the official car that would convey him to the hotel, Jerry Barton prepared to begin his search for Miow. He managed to unearth Sumet on Krabi who told him of having hidden Miow in the *horng* and of the trips that were made to take food and water to her. He said that he would have offered to take Jerry there, but a fisherman had come in to say that he had seen a yacht not far from the *horngs* pick up someone from the sea who resembled Miow. "They were *farang,* he said, who appeared to be scuba diving nearby", Sumet told Jerry.

Later, discussing matters with the men from the DEA and comparing notes, Jerry discovered that some Americans were involved in Khun Pho's operations. "We have been suspicious of them for some time," said Dillon Hart, the Drug Enforcement man, "they look and behave like your typical out for a good time young American tourist, personable looking guys with some nice looking American gals, but we have reason to believe that two of them at least are not quite what they seem."

"I have reason to believe that Miow was picked up by some *farang* scuba diving from their yacht", Jerry informed them.

"It could be our guys", said Vincent Maclain, another of the DEA team, "that's their modus operandi, happy and healthy tourists enjoying the beauty of Phuket."

"Then we must get hold of them before they do something terrible, they may have Miow with them or they may know where she is."

The two Americans exchanged glances and looked uncomfortable. Jerry caught the look and interpreted it correctly. "You mean you can't do anything to save Miow?" he demanded, then as Dillon nodded his head and looked rueful, he exploded: "well, that's unacceptable. I shall have to go after them myself and I give you fair warning that my colleague Miow is my first priority."

Vince Maclain intervened: "Of course we understand how you feel, but I'm sorry, it's no go. We've had our eyes trained on these guys for months, we know they will lead us to Pho and there's no way we're going to let you jeopardise that."

Jerry glared at them before he strode from the room. He had to go it alone and that was what he would do. There was no question of going after the smugglers before ensuring Miow's safety. He appreciated the DEA men's position but it was not one he could adopt. Miow's safety came before any other consideration and he was going to make damned certain of that.

After Barton had left the room, the DEA men looked at each other, then Vince Maclain shrugged and said: "He's gotta be stopped. Better get someone to shadow him so we know what he gets up to."

Jerry was smouldering with anger; his insides felt churned up with anxiety, irritation and an awful sense of *deja vu*. He told himself: 'You have to pull yourself together Jerry my lad, this just won't do. Think clearly now, what's the first thing to do?' He decided that his best bet would be to try and locate the Americans who had supposedly rescued Miow from the sea. Even as the thought crossed his mind, Vince was saying to Dillon: "He will probably try and find our guys and that has to be stopped at all costs. He mustn't be allowed anywhere near them."

Jerry made his way to the Yacht Club where the regatta was in full swing.

He picked his way among the crowds of people:

sailing crews animatedly discussing the day's racing, sightseers and well-wishers, friends, enjoying the amenities of the club while they waited for the next race to commence. Jerry noted that Marcus Stone was nowhere in sight but he continued to move among the crowd looking for two American men, probably accompanied by a couple of good looking girls.

As he picked his way between the tables, a girl sitting at the bar with her companions, remarked to her girl friend: "Hey, get a load of that guy, looks like a thundercloud, but Jeez is he handsome!"

Instantly, the heads of her male escorts swivelled round. "That's Barton of the Brit embassy", Tony hissed at Greg. "Remember to be very careful, better leave all the talking to me."

"So what's new?" said Greg disgustedly.

Neither Jerry nor the Americans were aware of the DEA's men following Jerry in order to prevent a meeting between them. As Barton approached the bar, a man carrying drinks came up to him and knocking against him, spilled a large quantity of liquid all over him. "I'm so sorry," he apologised, "here, let me help you. No, no, you must let me, I'm so sorry, really."

"That's all right, never mind", said Jerry, curbing his irritation with difficulty, but the other man was insistently solicitous and by the time he had extricated himself, he noticed that the group sitting at the bar had vanished. His clothes were wet and he smelled like a badly mixed cocktail so he decided to go back to his hotel and change before trying once more to track down his quarry.

Miow, meanwhile, was trying to keep a low profile in order to evade Pho's henchmen, while at the same time she set about the task of locating Jerry Barton. All her attempts drew a blank because Jerry had not yet checked in at the hotel. "We have a booking for the

British embassy", said the receptionist at the hotel, "but we don't have any names."

Turning away, wondering what to do next, Miow saw Marcus Stone crossing the lobby. She had no idea about his change of heart and so she quickly decided that her best course of action would be to follow him, he might lead her to where the drop was to be made.

Following someone is not easy, but it was made less difficult for Miow because she was able to blend in to her surroundings. A pretty young Thai woman strolling along did not arouse any curiosity beyond an admiring glance or two.

It soon became clear that Stone was headed for the yacht club. He walked along jauntily, a spring in his step. Miow thought bitterly: 'what's **he** got to be so happy about? He's about to ruin the lives of so many people with those drugs and he doesn't even need the money!'

Marcus Stone never looked back once, he had no need to for his conscience was clear, he had nothing more to worry about than the next race. He feared no repercussions because he was sure that the British embassy would give him protection, he would fly out as soon as the race was over and then the British police would take over to protect him and his family if the need arose. Meanwhile, he was going to win the race, he was sure of it and life was good again.

Jerry Barton, returning to check into the hotel, was told by the receptionist that a Thai lady had been enquiring for him. His heart leapt, it must have been Miow.

"What did she look like? What did she say?" he demanded.

The receptionist smiled coyly: "She velly pletty", she answered, "velly disappointed I tell her you not check in yet."

"Do you know where she went?" Jerry asked, even as he realised the futility of the question.

But he reckoned without the receptionist's desire to be helpful in what she scented to be a romance.

"She look sad but then her face change, she go out behind him."

"Him? Whom?"

"I not see too proper but it maybe could be Mr Stone."

"Did she talk to him? Could you hear what she said?" Jerry could not conceal his excitement.

"No, no, she go out behind him", the girl repeated.

Could this mean Miow had decided to shadow Stone? Thanking the receptionist, Jerry made his way to his room where he showered and changed his clothes before hurrying out of the hotel. Perhaps Marcus Stone had gone to the Yacht Club....he decided to go back there himself to look for both of them: Miow and Marcus.

CHAPTER FIFTEEN

Miow, following discreetly behind Marcus Stone, could not help being surprised by his jaunty air and total disregard of his surroundings. He did not look like a man who has something to hide, one engaged in dangerous clandestine activity. Clearly, he was totally unaware that she was tailing him and as they proceeded it became obvious that Stone was bound for the Yacht Club.

Tony and Greg, having dropped their girls off at the BoatHouse Hotel, proceeded to their apartment on Kata beach.

"Obviously", said Tony, "that Barton character was looking for someone and my guess is it was us. Damn it to hell! This is one time we can't afford to lay low and hibernate. How in hell did he get on to us?"

"We don't know that for sure", Greg was placatory, "we can't assume he's on to us."

"We can't afford not to assume it," Tony snapped, "we can't afford to get complacent, not at this or any stage of the game."

"What I wonder", Greg said, still placatory, "is who the guy was that spilled the drinks on Barton. From where I was sitting it looked quite deliberate."

Tony looked at him with interest. "Now there's a thought...the plot thickens. He was no one I recognised, he's definitely not from Pho's outfit, though of course, he could be a local who was pressed into service. Hmm, I wonder, maybe the drink was spilled to prevent Barton from talking to us, in which case it could only be on the orders of Pho or his men."

"Shouldn't we get in touch with Lek or Nok?" queried Greg.

"Yeah, that's exactly what I'm about to do" and

Tony went to the telephone and rapidly dialled a number. He spoke in fluent Thai and Greg who had mastered only the basics of the language could not follow the entire conversation. When Tony had replaced the receiver, Greg looked at him expectantly. Tony was frowning horribly and he shook his head. "Lek knows nothing about the guy at the Club. He knows Barton and the Ambassador have arrived and he says we have to move quickly now. He's all set to have Stone make the drop and be picked up by the police while we sail away with the goods. Still, I'm worried about that guy..."

"Maybe it was just an accident, kind of thing that happens all the time", Greg said.

"Maybe", Tony agreed, "but it's a coincidence and I don't trust coincidences. And I haven't worked out yet what that little cat was doing in the water when we picked her up and how she fits into all this. I'd surely like to get my hands on her."

Jerry, meanwhile made his way back to the Club and the first thing he noticed was that the man who had spilled the drinks on him was no longer there. Did that mean anything? Perhaps not, perhaps it had been a coincidence, but Jerry like Tony, did not trust coincidences. He looked around and there among the crowds of laughing happy people was Marcus Stone. Jerry's lips tightened at the sight of the famous yachtsman who was talking and laughing with his crew. Swivelling round, Jerry drew in his breath sharply, for among the shadows at the far corner he was sure he had seen Miow.

By the time he reached the area where he had seen her, Miow had disappeared. Cursing softly, Jerry retraced his steps back into the bar area where Marcus Stone continued to chat with his cronies. Jerry seated himself at the bar and ordered a drink. He waited to see what Stone would do. Soon enough, he made his way to the bar and said with a laugh: "Another round, please."

Jerry said evenly: "You appear to be in a very good mood, Mr Stone."

Marcus laughed and picked up his bottle of beer, saying as he did so: "I am indeed" and then he turned. His eyes widened in surprise and he set the bottle down again and extended his hand.

"Mr Barton, I think? I have been trying to get you at the embassy and they never told me you were here in Phuket."

"Well", said Jerry coldly, although he shook the proffered hand, "the embassy does not usually hand out information."

"Anyway, I am so glad to see you. I have a great deal to tell you and we cannot talk here. Is there somewhere quiet where we can meet?"

Jerry was puzzled, he had certainly not expected this; was the man bluffing? He certainly seemed sincere enough.

"We can meet at my hotel in half an hour if that will suit you", he said.

"It will indeed. I shall finish my drink and tell my chaps that I am off and then I'll be there."

Miow had decided that as Marcus Stone was safely ensconced at the club with his crew members, she could afford to take off and resume her search for Jerry. She walked back to the hotel and went up to the receptionist. As soon as the girl saw Miow she beamed and said: "Mr Barton, he check in already and I tell him you ask for him." Then relapsing into Thai she added: "He was very upset, I could see, that he had missed you."

"Where is he now?" Miow asked and could not help

showing her happiness and relief.

The helpful receptionist smiled back at her: "I told him you went out after Mr Stone and he did not like that at all, I could see."

"Yes, but where is he now?"

The girl was crestfallen, she would have dearly liked to be able to bear good news. "I don't know", she admitted reluctantly, "he just went out."

Enough, thought Miow, no more of this running around, I'm just going to sit here and wait for him. She seated herself in the lobby from where she could keep an eye on the entrance and before too long she was rewarded by the sight of Jerry striding in. Miow jumped up and as Jerry caught sight of her there was such a look of pure love on his face that Miow caught her breath and without a second thought went straight into his arms. They stood there like that for a moment, unmoving, lost to the world around them and then Jerry let his arms drop and Miow moved back.

"Thank god you're safe", said Jerry, "I've been having such nightmares since you disappeared.."

"Oh Jerry, they made a fool out of me, making me hide out on Krabi. And I lost my cell phone and couldn't contact you.." Miow interrupted him.

Jerry broke in: "What happened?"

"I swam out to a yacht and nearly drowned but some Americans on it saved me and brought me back to Phuket."

"I know, a fisherman told Sumet he had seen you being picked up. I went there looking for you. But where are those Americans, do you know anything about them?"

"No, no, I don't," Miow replied, "but one of the men was rather edgy and very annoyed because I wouldn't tell him anything."

Jerry explained to her then what the DEA had told

him about some Americans who were working for Pho and who were known to be in Phuket pretending to be part of the sailing fraternity. It came to him then that the man who had spilled the drinks on him had probably been sent by the DEA chaps to prevent him from effecting a meeting with them.

Jerry then told Miow of his meeting with Stone. "He should be here any minute, he actually seemed pleased to see me and asked if he could talk to me in private."

Miow was as puzzled as Jerry had been. "That's odd, isn't it?" she mused, "do you think he's trying to hoodwink us somehow?"

"The thought crossed my mind", Jerry said drily, "but all will soon be revealed for here comes the gentleman in question now."

Marcus Stone joined them and Jerry introduced him to Miow. "This is my colleague Sukanya Limthongkul", he said gravely.

Miow looked carefully at Stone, then extended her hand and said: "Please call me Miow, everybody does."

Mr Stone smiled. "And I'm Marcus."

Jerry was unsmiling as he said: "Shall we go up to my room? I think you said you have something you want to discuss?"

Once inside the room, Marcus Stone burst almost immediately into speech. "You cannot imagine the relief of this meeting", he said, "I tried calling the embassy but, as I explained, could not get through to you."

"Mr. Stone", Jerry's face matched the grimness of his tone, "I think we should cut the cackle and get down to exactly what it is you want to say."

"Yes, of course", Marcus responded, "I don't know how much you know but until very recently I was part of a plot, a sinister and awful plot. There are things in everybody's lives that they are ashamed of or need to hide. There was such an incident in mine and these people somehow got hold of it. I was blackmailed into agreeing to carry drugs back to the UK on my yacht. But I could not go through with it although they threatened the lives of my wife and child. I have called home and made arrangements for my family's safety, I have spoken to my sponsors and told them the truth and I tried to call you to tell you what was going on."

There was a silence as the three regarded each other, trying to read one another's expressions and to get at the final truth behind the spoken words.

It was Miow who spoke first. "I'm so glad!" she exclaimed impulsively, "we just couldn't imagine how or why someone like you would be involved in something so sordid."

Marcus smiled sadly. "Yes, well..." he began.

Jerry Barton cut in. "We will need a bit more than you have told us", he said, "we need names, dates, places."

Marcus then told them of the plan, of the pick up he was expected to make on Hu Min Sang. He described Khun Lek and Jerry knew at once that he was one of Khun Pho's principal henchmen.

"What I don't understand", he said, thinking aloud, "is where the Americans come in, the ones the DEA is watching, the chaps who picked you up", he added to Miow.

Miow shrugged and then explained to Marcus about her hideaway, her escape and her rescue by the Americans in their yacht. Marcus Stone looked perplexed.

"I can't help with that, I'm afraid, I never met any Americans."

Jerry frowned and Miow could tell that he was thinking furiously.

"Why would they want to use someone like you,

Stone? Why was the body put in the lake and what is the connection with the Ploenchit Fair? And if, as the DEA believes, the Americans are involved where do they fit in? Answer those questions and we'll have solved it."

This time it was Marcus Stone who shrugged. Miow stared for a moment at Jerry then she spoke, her voice doubtful.

"Could it be that Mr Stone, Marcus, was being used as a sort of blind, a decoy or something?"

"By George!" said Jerry, "I think you may have got it! But that still doesn't entirely explain the elaborate Ploenchit charade, not to mention the death of that poor unfortunate girl."

"That was to make you think it was me, to throw you off the scent, kind of like a threat, maybe", Miow spoke fast, excited by the puzzle she was attempting to solve. "Then while they had me in self-imposed hiding, Marcus here would make the pick up while somewhere else the real pick up was taking place."

"Well," said Jerry, "I think you've hit on something there. Yes, that's a distinct possibility and would make some sense out of all the senseless things that have been happening. If we agree on this hypothesis we have to discover exactly where and how the real pick up is going to be made. If, as we believe, the Americans are involved, then we have to get on to them straightaway and how are we going to do that?"

There was a momentary silence and the three of them regarded each other, each one busy with their own thoughts. Then Miow said: "I think the only possible way is for me to go back to them with some story or other and try and find out what they are up to."

"Impossible"! Jerry exploded, "that's dangerous and you know it. I cannot and will not allow it."

"You can't stop me", Miow retorted, " in any case,

what other alternative is there? Or are you going to let them get away with it?"

"It does seem the only way", Marcus Stone put in tentatively, "I agree it's very dangerous but maybe we can provide some sort of back-up to protect her. I'd be more than willing to do whatever I can.."

"I think this is the DEA's pigeon," said Jerry, "I am going to talk to Vince Maclain and see what he comes up with". Saying which, he strode to the telephone and dialled.

Miow poured herself a mineral water and offered Marcus a beer; meanwhile, she was busily concocting her own plan. She decided that she would go to Greg and Tony and tell them that she was tired of being just a low paid employee of the embassy and that she wanted a share of the pickings. She might even suggest that she had met Marcus Stone and got involved with him...the ideas ran through her fertile imagination and she longed to be up and doing.

Jerry replaced the receiver and came back into the room.

"The DEA has no idea which of the many Americans on Phuket might be Khun Pho's people. They have their suspicions, they say, but no more than that. Frankly, I think they just don't want us in on it at this point."

"Then", said Miow, "the only way to find out is to let me get close to Tony and Greg. Then we can find out if they are what they seem to be and eliminate them from the enquiry."

"I was supposed to make the pick up on the second last day of the Regatta", Marcus Stone interposed, "that doesn't give us much time."

"Well", said Miow when Jerry still did not speak, "my money is on Tony and Greg. I was uneasy about that Tony, there was something about him, call it my female instinct."

Jerry Barton was obviously troubled. "How will you go about it?" he asked Miow, then added: "It's bloody dangerous, especially if they have the slightest inkling of who you really are."

"I'm sure they don't", Miow replied with cheerful assurance, "how could they? They fished me up out of the sea and I told them nothing at all." She suppressed the fact that Tony had been annoyed, that he had been both suspicious and interested and a shiver ran through her.

"Don't underestimate them", said Jerry, as if reading her mind, "it could be fatal."

Jerry had to fight his instinct to protect Miow and keep her safe. She was his colleague and there was a job of work to be done. In any case, he knew, Miow would resent any attempt by him to protect her.

Together they began to plan their strategy; listening to them, Marcus Stone felt admiration for their professionalism.

It was decided that Miow would go back to the two Americans she knew as Tony and Greg to try and inveigle herself into their good graces. She would offer to work with them. "For", said Jerry, "it's more than likely (if they are who and what we think) that they know who you are, so there would be no point in pretending to be a damsel in distress or having fallen for Tony's blue eyes!"

"Brown, actually" and Miow dimpled mischievously.

CHAPTER SIXTEEN

Miow went back to the Yacht Club and as luck was with her, the very first person she saw was Greg. She was glad because, although she had not admitted this to Jerry, she was a little intimidated by Tony. There was something sinister about him, even his smile.

"Well, hi there!" Greg called, "good to see you again, Ms Cat, hope you're none the worse for your little adventure?"

Miow pretended to be surprised to see him, then looking around conspiratorially, she whispered: "Am I glad to see you! I was actually hoping I'd run into you."

Now it was Greg's turn to look surprised. "Oh," he said "and why would that be, or were you in a hurry to return Sara's T shirt and stuff?"

Miow cursed herself for not thinking of this very simple ploy to renew their acquaintance; she had been so busy trying to find Jerry that the borrowed clothes had quite escaped her memory.

"Yes", she replied, "and I wanted to thank you for all your help. I know your friend thought me rude not to have trusted you with my story. I couldn't then but now I would like to."

"Is that right?" Greg thought what a feather in his cap it would be if he could bring information to Tony.

"Yes, but we can't talk here, I shouldn't even be seen with you. Can we go somewhere private?"

"Come with me", said Greg with mock courtesy and offered his arm.

Watching through binoculars from his car, Jerry Barton turned to Marcus Stone.

"She's got him". To himself he added: 'pray they don't get her!'

88

When Tony came forward and took her by the hand, Miow could not entirely suppress the shiver of alarm that ran through her as he touched her; there was something about him that she sensed behind his urbane manner, a menace and a ruthlessness. He was the dangerous one, she decided, Greg was much less frightening.

"Not afraid of me, surely? Or is it the sea air?" Tony was enjoying himself, Miow thought, he was like a sleek and well fed cat toying with a mouse.

"Should I be afraid of you?" she asked lightly and looked up at him flirtatiously.

"Not unless you're a naughty girl", he responded with a laugh that chilled Miow's blood. "I'm very good to good girls, right Tony? And now lets hear what brings you here."

Miow looked him straight in the eye, willing herself to show no fear.

"I want to join you, to work with you", she blurted, "I'm fed up of the Brits, I get to do all the dirty work and there are no rewards. That Jerry Barton treats me like some inferior subordinate, yet it's me that takes all the risks." She hoped this sounded convincing.

"And what work is it you think we're doing"? Tony asked.

"Well, I have to confess that I guessed you weren't just yachtsmen out for a sail. As you may know, we work closely with the DEA and you sort of fit a description they gave us." Miow studied Tony's face, wondering if she was on the right tack.

'So', thought Tony, 'I was right and the DEA is on to us. Now how do I use this woman to save our skin?'

Aloud, he said: "I don't quite follow you. What is it you think you can do for us and why would you want to?"

'He's no fool', thought Miow, 'as if I didn't know.

Now how do I get him to believe me?'

Aloud, she said: "I told you. I'm fed up of taking all the risks, doing all the dirty work and earning a pittance while Jerry Barton swans around with the ambassador. Money is the name of the game and its what I want. As to what I can do for you, you tell me, but I know there's a big drop coming up."

Tony exchanged glances with Greg. "There is indeed," Tony said, "and your Brit pal the famous yachtsman Marcus Stone is scheduled to pick it up."

Miow hesitated. Was she supposed to know this and if so, was she also supposed to know that the real drop did not involve Stone? Perhaps, anyway, she had better not let on that she knew Stone had reneged. She decided to take a chance on it.

"The embassy knows about Stone's involvement but I believe the real drop is going to take place somewhere else. Why on earth would Khun Pho want to use someone as public as Marcus Stone? That's what **I** have been asking myself."

"Clever little Miss Cat", and as always there was that thread of menace running through the silk of his voice, "you are quite right, **we** are about to make the pick up ourselves before we sail off into the blue."

Miow knew better than to utter the where and when that rose to her lips. She had still, she knew, to allay suspicion and she sensed that they, Tony certainly, did not trust her. This being so, she asked herself, why had he confided that Marcus Stone was a decoy and that he himself was the smuggler?

As if aware of her thoughts, Tony came close to her and whispered:

"Well, now that you know, you also know that there's no way you can get off this boat, don't you? You're here to stay for the duration" and he laughed unpleasantly.

Miow forced herself to smile back at him. "No problem", she said, "I want to be a part of your operation, I told you, I'm totally fed up of the British embassy."

"Well, this is your big chance", Tony replied, "but first you'll have to do something to prove your good faith." He looked at her keenly as he spoke and Miow prayed that he could not read her mind with his penetrating gaze.

She looked back at him with what she hoped was an innocent expression and asked: "What is it? Tell me what you want me to do and if it is humanly possible, I promise I'll do it."

"Isn't she an eager beaver, Greg?" Tony laughed and Miow thought to herself that although he seemed to laugh such a lot, she had never heard such a mirthless sound. "What we want you to do is to kill Jerry Barton and frame our fine friend Marcus Stone. That should kill two birds with one stone, give everyone plenty to occupy them and take the heat off us while we sail out of here with the goods."

Miow suppressed the gasp that rose to her lips. This was totally unexpected and she had no idea how she was going to deal with this new situation; she knew, however, that she must not show her confusion and dismay. She assumed an insouciant expression and asked: "How am I supposed to do this if I'm not allowed off this boat?"

Don't you worry about that, little puss", Tony smiled mirthlessly, "you will have someone with you who won't hesitate to do what he does best if you try any kind of double cross" and he drew a hand across his throat. "Call it insurance so we can let you off this boat and see if we can trust you".

Miow was at complete loss; they had really managed to spike her guns and she had no idea what to do next. She knew she could not warn Jerry and she certainly could not approach Marcus Stone because Tony and Greg were watching her. What on earth was she to do?

Tony had been watching her and now he laughed his mirthless laugh. "Can't see your way to doing it, can you, Miss Cat?" he jeered. "What shall we do with her Greg? You got any good ideas, apart from the obvious which I know you would dearly like to do?"

"Don't be in such a hurry to write me off, " Miow retorted with a bravado she didn't feel. "I'm just thinking things through. I don't just rush into things even if you do.."

Good for you but we don't have much time so you had better come up with something like pronto, know what I mean?"

Miow nodded, she could not trust herself to speak just then. In any case, what could she say when she did not have even the ghost of an idea of how she was going to proceed.

CHAPTER SEVENTEEN

Jerry Barton and Marcus Stone were waiting and watching; there was little else they could do at this stage as they waited to hear from Miow. Jerry paced the room, unable to deal with the forced inactivity. If he could have stopped Miow he would have done so but she was her own person and determined to do what she deemed necessary.

While they waited, Stone tried to engage Jerry in conversation, aware of the other man's tension. They chatted, discovering much in common and Jerry was glad that Stone had not turned out to be the drug smuggler they had thought he might be.

Not unnaturally, Marcus Stone showed a great deal of interest in the whole question of drugs and smuggling. "How do they recruit couriers?" he asked.

"Usually they are young foreigners, someone who's run out of money or who likes a bit of danger and is tempted by huge sums of money. They are usually to be found in cheap guesthouses in Bangkok, Pattaya and Phuket. The other kind of courier, Thai and Chinese are a whole different kettle of fish. That's their way of life, they are organized, have false papers and travel a great deal. They are well aware of the risk but it is worth it at about $2000 a kilogram."

"But what happens if they get caught? Isn't there a death sentence here?"

"If they get caught their families are taken care of by the drug barons, a sort of insurance plan, especially if they do not squeal. And although there is a death sentence, it is usually commuted to a life sentence."

"How do they catch drug smugglers? Do they use x-ray machines? I've never seen sniffer dogs like they have in Oz."

"Good intelligence work mainly. Known suppliers are kept under police surveillance and there is a large network of informers. What the casual drug smuggler does not realize is that almost as soon as he has bought his stash, the seller informs the authorities..Once at the airport, they just check out the traveler who best fits the profile of a typical courier: usually but not always male,, someone in their twenties or thirties, travelling alone with hand luggage and a whole lot of visas."

Jerry then moved over to the desk on which stood a small machine.. "I think we should be picking up something now," he said and turned on the machine. The red light glowed before settling into a bright green spot. Unbeknownst to Miow, Jerry had placed a listening device in the depths of her handbag and they would be able to hear every word that was spoken on that boat. Jerry was pale, his face drawn as he crouched over the machine, swearing softly under his breath. Marcus went up to him and placed a hand on his shoulder. "Try and relax old chap. You have to admire her courage and her poise, she knows what she's doing."

"Does she? I don't think so. She's just feeling her way and meanwhile she is in terrible danger." He held up his hand to forestall Stone's response. Loud and clear, they heard Tony's outrageous proposal that Miow should kill Jerry and frame Marcus as a drug smuggler trying to get away with the goods.

"Bloody hell!" Marcus mouthed the words. Jerry still had his arm outstretched in a silencing gesture while he listened intently to the disembodied voices that reached them from the depths of Miow's handbag.

When it became clear that the recording had stopped, Jerry ceased his pacing and came up to where Marcus was standing, a horrified expression on his face.

"What in hell are we going to do? I am to be killed by Miow and you are to be framed for the murder! Of course, there are all kinds of things we can do to throw them off and to extricate Miow, but that would mean we wouldn't get our quarry and right at this moment that is my number one priority....that and Miow's safety, he added hastily.

"Of course", Marcus assented. "I for one, cannot wait to get the men who set all this up, caused me so much grief. But as you say, what in hell are we going to do about it? I mean, for instance, could we use this tape?" he nodded towards the gadget lying on the table.

"Not really. They could deny the whole thing and we might be guilty of entrapment. In any case, they would go free as no crime will have been committed, so we would not be able to nail them." Jerry strode up an down the room, then paused and turned towards Marcus. "We could let them carry out their plan, or SEEM to carry out their plan, and then nab them; but that would mean getting hold of Miow and I don't see how we are going to do that since they are hardly likely to let her out of their sight." Jerry was frowning horribly as he concentrated on the problem.

Stone, too, was thinking hard. "What about we let her think she's going to have to do it? They can hardly stand over her as she plunges in the knife or shoots a gun.."

"That's true," Jerry conceded, "but the problem will be to get her to that point. She is never going to agree to their suggestion and where does that leave her? Hopefully, she will play for time and they will go along with it."

Miow was coming to the same idea. What, she asked herself, was to prevent her from pretending to do the killing? Inwardly, she shuddered at the very idea of

Jerry being murdered. After all, she reasoned with herself, neither Tony nor Greg could possibly be with her inside the room when she actually did the deed. She could alert Jerry and explain the whole situation to him and the smugglers could be nabbed. What bothered her was that Tony and Greg were not the major players. Getting them would not necessarily mean they would get the really big fish like Khun Pho who would swim away to safety.. Unless…..Could she possibly manage to get that information out of one or other of the two men before she agreed to do their dirty work? She rather doubted if she could get anything out of Tony because he was obviously a hard nut to crack, but Greg might well be easier to manipulate and he had an eye for a pretty woman. Yes, the more she thought about it, the more the idea appealed to her.

They had of course taken away her mobile phone before incarcerating her on the boat and she had no means of contacting Jerry.

Tony and Greg, meanwhile, were having their own discussion. "Do you really think she will do it?" Greg asked.

"Her boss's murder?" Tony smiled in his sinister way, " Not bloody likely! That girl is up to something and I sure as hell do not buy her little act of wanting out of the embassy and in with us, unless she's fallen for your blue eyes. No, I don't buy any of it but I am willing to use her for own purposes, so just you make sure you do not let her out of your sight."

CHAPTER EIGHTEEN

Miow approached Greg where he sat on the deck of the boat cleaning some fish he had caught. He looked up at her and smiled, shading his eyes from the sun. "Going somewhere?" he asked, "If so, I'll just finish this little lot and come with you?"

"Don't trust me, do you?" Miow smiled back.

"Can you blame me?" Greg countered, "anyway, what do you want to do that you can't do with me?"

"Kill Jerry. Forinstance? You can hardly stand over me while I do that, can you?"

"No," he agreed amiably, "but I can stand just outside and make sure you are doing what you should".

"True. Obviously you are afraid of your boss; no, not Tony, I mean your real boss. A real meanie, is he?"

"I don't know what you are talking about," said Greg and his voice had changed, lost its air of good humour."

"Oh yes you do, Greg. Come on, tell me. After all, if I'm working with you and hell, it's me that's sticking her neck out, I should at least have the whole picture."

"What makes you think it's not Tony, or me for that matter?" But Greg's voice lacked conviction and Miow thought she might be winning.

"Because it is obvious, Greg, is why. I can see how he bosses you around but he's a hired hand if ever there was one. I can tell."

"Yes, well, that is all I know too." A sulky expression settled on Greg's face; he had not liked her reference to Tony bossing over him..

"What about Khun Pho?" Miow asked, "in fact you needn't bother to deny it because the embassy knows it."

'Well,' Greg thought to himself, 'I suppose that's

true and anyway, what can she do about it?' It pleased him to be able to say that Tony was not the kingpin, even if he acted like he was.

"OK", he said, "maybe you are right. Khun Pho could be the big boss."

"I knew that," Miow said airily, "but what I don't understand is this elaborate charade with Stone."

"I'm not sure but I have heard that Khun Pho hates white people especially the Brits, but don't ask me why. Maybe something that happened to him way back when, loss of face and all that, you know the sort of thing."

"That figures," said Miow slowly, working it out, "all that motiveless malignity doesn't wash somehow, but a spot of revenge spicing up a profitable deal, laughing at one's hapless enemies, that makes very good sense."

"Well now, what about a little plan to deal with OUR hapless enemies. What are you going to do about Barton and co.?"

"I don't want to kill anyone, that's for sure, it's not my thing, but if that is what it takes, I will do it", Miow replied, looking Greg straight in the eye. Inwardly, her mind was seething . "Now I have to plan the where and the when".

"Not much time left, my lovely, no time to hang about, it's today or not at all." Tony's voice was jeering, he had joined them soundlessly and Miow noticed that his sandals were rubber soled.. "Both Barton and Stone are in their hotel and now is the time, so go for it little cat and you, Greg, stick close to her. The killing has to be done before the start of Stone's next race. When the deed is done, come back and report.. I will make arrangements for Stone to be picked up for the murder. We could have him dispatched along with Barton, but that is not what Khun Pho wants."

As Miow and Greg left the deck, Tony called Greg back and whispered in his ear and they both smiled evilly. Miow shuddered.

CHAPTER NINETEEN

Jerry Barton and Marcus Stone had, of course, overheard this conversation on their listening device.

"Well now," said Jerry, "we've got them admitting to murder and that Khun Pho, as we suspected, is behind the whole thing."

"But will that be proof enough?" Marcus countered. "I mean how reliable is this man as a witness and what is to prevent everyone from denying everything? I mean, those voices are none too clear and there is a lot of static or something."

"Unfortunately, you are right, but it could serve as supplementary evidence once we have the villains banged up tp rights. And that is the next step."

Had anyone observed the two men in the next half hour or so, they would have had serious doubts about their sanity. Feverishly, Barton and Stone set to work; there was little conversation between them as they moved about the room arranging things. Then they stood back and surveyed their handiwork.

"Very realistic," said Marcus, "couldn't tell it from the real thing...or should I say person?"

Jerry smiled. "Lets hope it serves its purpose. But we also have to hope Miow won't be alone, that they will send someone with her. Otherwise, it's no good, it will all be in vain."

"Well, we shall just have to wait and see," Stone replied, "no good anticipating the worst, lets just hope for the best outcome. Hell!" he added, "I cannot believe that this is happening, but then everything about my life recently has been totally unreal."

Jerry nodded sympathetically. "Yes, I know, this must be hell for you. Let us hope it will soon be ended and that you can go back to the real world. Now I have to make sure that my friend Vichai has arrived with back-up."

The conversation on his mobile was short but obviously satisfactory. "He's here", Jerry said tersely, "and he is ready to move."

It was time for Stone and Barton to go their separate ways and carry out what they had planned, hoping against hope that with all the intangible elements of the case, things would go as they wished.

Marcus Stone went back to the club to get ready for the race; as things stood, he knew that he was not expected to complete it because when according to his instructions, he took the drugs on board his boat at Hin Mu Sang, he would be arrested by the police who would be waiting for him. What would happen, he asked himself, if Barton did get accidentally knocked off by Miow or the men she was pretending to work with and was unable to rescue him? He shuddered at the thought. 'No,' he said firmly to himself, 'I must not think like that. It has to succeed, we have to win'. He shivered again and said to himself: 'Just an old goose walking over my grave.'

Marcus was greeted by his crew who were waiting for him, unaware of his predicament, and they were soon deep in the preparations for the race and there was no more time to think of anything else. Marcus Stone was once more the professional yachtsman preparing for a major race.

Jerry Barton, meanwhile, made several more calls on his mobile. He wondered how Miow was and whether she was afraid or her usual insouciant self. As the evening wore on, he made himself as conspicuous as possible, talking to several people, complaining about his dinner, drawing attention to himself. Then he went back to his room, unlocked the door and made sure that no one had entered the room in his absence.

He opened the wardrobe and climbed in; with the door slightly ajar, he had a good view of the room, especially the desk and chair and the occupant of the chair. He settled down to an uncertain vigil and hoped he wouldn't be too stiff at the end of it. His lips curved in a grim smile: 'just hope I won't be a stiff at the end of it!'

While he waited in the wardrobe, cautiously flexing his muscles as often as he could, Jerry's thoughts turned to Miow. What guts the girl had! He could not imagine many women who would have undertaken what she had…would Suzy have been capable of it? He rather doubted it, not because Suzy had not been brave but because…had Suzy been brave? Taking an overdose of drugs was not the act of a brave person. For the first time since that long ago tragedy in Oxford, Jerry faced up to the flaw in Suzy's character that had made her, in the first instance, vulnerable to drugs and secondly to her desperate act of suicide. It did not in any way change his implacable hatred of the men who peddled drugs, battening on the weakness of the young and vulnerable, but for the first time he felt able to let Suzy go, to set himself and her spirit free

'And now', Jerry said wryly to himself, " here I am, hiding in a cupboard, waiting for the woman I love to come in and try to kill me!'

He knew that Inspector Vichai and his men would have taken up their position around and within the hotel room. Vichai had admitted that he was not wildly enthusiastic about the plan that Jerry had unfolded to him. There would be a hell of a lot of explaining to do to account for Miow Limthongkul's presence in that room armed with a knife, trying to kill a senior British diplomat who was her boss.

What on earth had persuaded her to participate in

such a wild scheme? Vichai had to admit that he admired Miow's courage and resourcefulness, but the Lord knew he would not want any woman of his to be involved in such a scheme. And then, thought Vichai, there was that chap Marcus Stone, how could an intelligent and highly placed man like that become involved in drugs and blackmail. And why had he not come clean at the outset? True, he said he had feared for his wife and child, but if only people had more faith in the police and the due processes of law, so much tragedy could be prevented; but, Vichai mused, we all have a fatal flaw, we all fear scandal, ridicule or disgrace, all sorts of imaginary fears and we so value public opinion, fickle and inconstant though we know it to be...

There was no obvious sound but Vichai stiffened and both he and Jerry in their respective hiding places knew that the door Vichai had closed behind him, had opened. They both heard keys jangling softly. Through the crack in the wardrobe Jerry watched as someone crept into the room. At the desk a man sat as if writing. The only light in the room came from a small table lamp that threw a circle of light on the papers lying on the desk, all else was in shadow.

Everyone, possibly even the intruder, held their breath and there was total silence in the room. The intruder paused for a moment by the door that had opened so soundlessly and then began to creep on stealthy feet towards the desk. The figure at the desk did not stir, seemingly engrossed in the papers spread out before him. He was sitting very still indeed and after a brief hesitation, the intruder continued at the speed of a snail to creep across the carpet, its deep pile absorbing his footfall.

Feeling that his lungs were bursting in the confined space of the wardrobe, Jerry cautiously let out a breath, slowly and soundlessly. He never took his eyes of that person creeping inexorably up to the seated figure at the desk. There was an inarticulate cry, something flashed in mid air and at the selfsame moment all the lights came on.

Jerry almost fell out of the wardrobe and Vichai was already at the desk, holding the arm of the intruder in a vice like grip. It was not Miow that Inspector Vichai held, it was an American who stood blinking in the light, the light revealing that the figure at the desk into whose back a knife had been plunged, was a dummy dressed to look like Jerry.

They stood there as if in a tableau and then turned as the door began to open slowly. Vichai and Jerry froze into stillness, waiting. The door opened fully and Miow stood there. Her eye went straight to the group around the desk and she gasped at the sight that met her. The figure at the desk had slumped forward and now lay across it, with his head on the papers before him and a knife sticking out of his back. Miow registered nothing else.

"Jerry, Jerry!" she cried, "I am too late, how could I let this happen?" She ran across the room and knelt by the figure. Then she looked up and a look of hate appeared on her face. "You will pay for this, Greg, you and Tony, you will pay dearly if it's the last thing I do."

The American smiled. "Oh, get real Miss Cat. Tony didn't trust you to pull it off and so I kinda anticipated, if you know what I mean. But that knife has your fingerprints all over it, not mine. But I guess you haven't tumbled to the fact that the 'body' is nothing but a dummy." He inclined his head to where Jerry stood.

Without a word, Miow rose from her knees and ran into Jerry's outstretched arms. "Thank God," she said fervently, "thank the Lord".

"Well", said Vichai, "good work all of you. We have the whole thing, the arrangement etc. on tape and this little 'murder' is on video. It may win no cinematic awards but it will help us get our chaps. Now lets have this fellow taken away and round up the rest."

CHAPTER TWENTY

Miow snuggled into Jerry's arms. "I'm so glad that's over, I just didn't know what to do."

"What were you planning to do?" Jerry enquired, "or were you planning to stick the knife in my ribs and explain afterwards?"

"Don't be funny," Miow pouted. Then she straightened up. "How did you know Greg (if that's his real name) and I were coming to kill you?" she asked.

"Elementary, my dear Watson, I planted a bug deep in the recesses of that holdall you call your bag before you went off to offer yourself as a would be assassin." The relief that it was over, that Miow was safe, was so great that Jerry could have broken down and wept.

"Less of the Watson, Sherlock Holmes," Miow responded in like vein, then she threw her arms around him again. "I'm so glad you did that."

"Me too," said Jerry, "otherwise I would have ended up dead and you would have been the murderer."

There was silence in the room for awhile as the couple sat entwined in each other's arms. Then Miow sat back and said: "What about Marcus and the drop?"

"Vichai will get that out of your friend Greg and they will all be picked up and there's an end." Jerry replied.

However, it was not to be so simple; they had reckoned without the wiliness of Khun Pho and his henchmen.

Marcus and his crew were on the boat, the Mark One, and they would soon be approaching Hin Mu Sang. Sweat broke out on Marcus Stone's forehead; was something going to happen here, he wondered, were the drugs actually on his beloved boat and if so, where had they been stashed? Had Jerry and Miow been able to forestall it? Thailand was not the sort of country in which you could be found with even a small amount of drugs. Marcus had heard that although the death penalty was rarely implemented, long terms of imprisonment are the norm. He knew that a sentence of 25 years was commonplace and Bangkok's jail, nicknamed the Hilton, was a place where no one in their right mind would want to end up.

Soon after the Mark One set out, Marcus noticed a police launch bearing down on them. As it came closer it sounded its siren and the wailing noise cut through the air with a dreadful melancholy. Marcus clenched and unclenched his fists and then he straightened up and stood tall.. He would, he decided in that moment, face whatever was in store with dignity. He was innocent, he told himself, therefore he had nothing to fear. Right? Wrong!, his inner voice told him, he was embroiled in a sinister plot and it was like a nightmare from which he could not wake.

The police loudhailer was calling his name now and Marcus automatically slowed the yacht and called to his crew to tack.

"What's up, Marcus? What are we doing?" they asked as he issued his commands. Marcus did not reply but his face was grim. Obviously, Jerry and Miow and that Thai policeman had been unable to come to his rescue and now, without their help, he told himself that he was for the chop.

The police boat came alongside and the Pol Cap requested permission to board the yacht. Curtly, Marcus responded in the affirmative and the policemen clambered on board, looking round them appreciatively as they did so. Pol Cap Manote, for it was he, asked to speak privately to Marcus.

"Now sir, no doubt you have least idea why we are

here?"

"You could say that," Marcus responded cautiously.

"We want," said the Pol Cap, lowering his voice conspiratorially, "that you deliver a package for us."

"What?" Marcus exploded, "no way, no packages, no delivery, not by me. You got that?"

"No, no, no, you not worry, no problem. Package already on boat and we use it to, how you say, catch mouse. We know every thing." As usual he turned all his r's into l's but Marcus was far from being amused.

"What mouse? I don't know what you are talking about." He was determined not to be tricked into any kind of admission.

Pol Cap Manote sighed theatrically. "You not afraiding," he said reassuringly, "all is known and these be Inspector Vichai's orders, he big time police chief from Krungthep, Bangkok. So, please you play game. Sail now to meeting place as arranged and we do the rest. All will be well, do not be worrying, sir." He then proceeded to tell Marcus where the drugs were stashed, in Marcus's own cabin.

"The bloody cheek of it!" Marcus exploded.

The policemen disembarked and the launch was soon out of sight, smacking the water as it sped off, rocking the yacht.

"Well," asked Chris Hampton, who with the rest of the crew had withdrawn while Marcus talked to the Pol Cap, "what was all that about and can we go now, we're losing precious time?"

"Yes," Marcus said, avoiding Chris's eyes, "on to Hin Mu Sang as per schedule." He did not look at his crew and vouchsafed no explanations. How and when, he wondered, had the drugs been placed on his beloved boat. 'God!' he thought, 'these people are devilish, will Jerry, Miow and the Inspector be able to circumvent them?' His not to question how; he had to play his part and sail to the rendezvous that had been arranged and hope it all worked out. Now that he knew the drugs were actually in his possession, he knew that he was in great danger if the slightest thing went wrong. And how far could he trust that Pol Cap, slimy bastard as he seemed? It was well known that the police not only turned a blind eye to the nefarious activities of rich and politically powerful gangsters, but actually assisted them, thereby reaping rich rewards which helped to eke out their meager salaries.

Well, it was too late to do anything about that.. Hin Mu Sang was coming into sight and the yacht tacked towards it. Almost instantly, three men jumped on board the Mark One. One was an America, the other two were Thais.

"Welcome," said the American, "hand over the goods like a good chap and then you can get under way." His smile was mocking.

Marcus threw the package at the man's feet and said tersely: "And now get off my boat before I throw you over."

"Temper, temper!" the American said mockingly, "but I think you have other visitors to delay you".

Marcus turned and saw the police launch. The Pol Cap grinned sheepishly at him. "Solly about it but I has my duty to do. I have to allest you for carrying velly big quantity drugs." He motioned to his henchmen who proceeded to handcuff Marcus.

Marcus was seething with rage; so after all, Jerry had not been able to rescue him. Where were they and what on earth was he going to do now? The idea of languishing in prison filled him with horror but he could see no help forthcoming. His mind raced: would Jerry be able to find him in jail? What had happened to Miow, had she somehow (unthinkably) killed Jerry and if so, why was she not with the American? Surely they would have used the opportunity to implicate her further? In any case, he thought, her presence or absence from the scene could not help him now. Should he attempt to bribe the grinning Pol Cap or would that land him in deeper shit?

The thoughts raced round his mind but he could think of no satisfactory solution or course of action. He was taken off the boat while his crew watched helplessly. As he lowered himself into the waiting police launch Marcus called up to them: "Go on with the race, I'll join you as soon as I can." The words sounded as empty to him as they probably did to them.

CHAPTER TWENTY-ONE

Meanwhile, Jerry, Miow and Vichai were congratulating themselves on the success of the sting. Greg had been marched away, alternately mouthing imprecations and pleading his innocence.

Vichai proceeded to explain what he had arranged.

"We arranged for your good friend Tony to go on Stone's yacht and take the drugs that had been placed there. Then the police boarded the vessel and arrested Marcus".

"But why?" asked Miow, "why didn't they arrest Tony?"

"So that Khun Pho and his American henchmen would think their plot had succeeded, that Marcus was arrested and they had got away with the loot."

"And?" Miow prompted him.

"And", replied Jerry, smiling fondly at her, "as soon as they landed with the drugs, Tony was arrested and will soon be joining his friend Greg."

"What about Khun Pho?" Miow enquired.

Jerry's face darkened and an expression of disgust crossed Vichai's usually inscrutable expression. "He has got away, of course, but for the last time, I promise you. We will surely get him next time I swear. The Americans will incriminate him and we know that Pol Cap Manote and others in the police are in his pay. He has a wide net but we will sweep it up eventually."

"It's always the way", said Miow, The big fish escape the net which catches the small fry".

"Well," said Jerry, "your Tony isn't such small fry. The DEA is very pleased to have caught him in their net, of that you may be very sure. I wish we lived in a different world but we do not. We can only do what we can, but be assured, no one is going to rest until we have the chap who is behind all this."

They all knew that money, power and ruthlessness protected the big players in the world of drugs smuggling. Too often, governments and police turned a blind eye for their share of one of the most lucrative businesses in the world. The stakes were high and so it goes on.

Looking at Jerry and his worried expression, knowing how much anger he felt against the drug lords, Miow snuggled up to him.

"Oh Jerry, I do love you", said Miow looking at him with all her love shining out her eyes. Jerry held her close, looking at her as if he could not believe what he saw.

And there, dear Reader, we must leave them.

Marcus Stone, released from his nightmare, returned to his boat and won the race. He returned to his beloved family and was a hero in more ways than one, fighting the drugs battle and trying in his own way to make the world a better place.

Lightning Source UK Ltd.
Milton Keynes UK
UKOW05f0256310714

236025UK00015B/41/P